TRUFFLES' DIARIES

TRUFFLES' DIARIES

The Memoirs and Mewsings of a Fat Tabby Cat

Sheila Collins

Foreword by Ann Widdecombe

APEX PUBLISHING LTD

First published in hardback in 2008, reprinted in paperback in 2016 by

Apex Publishing Ltd

12A St. John's Road, Clacton on Sea, Essex, CO15 4BP, United Kingdom

www.apexpublishing.co.uk

Copyright © 2008-2016 by Sheila Collins
The author has asserted her moral rights

British Library Cataloguing-in-Publication Data
A catalogue record for this book
is available from the British Library

ISBN: 978-1-78538-491-2

Typeset in 10.5pt Georgia

Cover Design: Siobhan Smith

Illustrations: Sheila Collins

FOREWORD

Anyone who has owned an ageing, fat, spoiled cat will immediately recognise the one in this book. Truffles is confident in her human slaves, snoozing on the sun warmed patio of her Cornish home and reminiscing about past events. When you read these feline memoirs, you will recognise some of the cast of four legged creatures but there are some new additions in the shape of several new kittens next door.

My own cats, Pugwash the Second and Arbuthnot would just love this book. What a pity they can't read - or then again perhaps not. They might learn too much about controlling humans!

Ann Widdecombe

Ann Widdecombe

www.apexpublishing.co.uk

TRUFFLES' DIARY

MAY I INTRODUCE MYSELF ...

Hello people, my name is Truffles and it seems pretty cool at the moment to write a diary - how popular are Bridget Jones and Adrian Mole? Before I start, though, just some background information so you will realise that I am, in fact, rather an important cat ...

I am now fifteen years and eleven months old, so I'm looking forward to a big celebration when, in a week from now, I reach the magic age of sixteen - roughly comparable to about eighty in human years. I'm pretty sure that my personal humans who look after me are planning something nice for the occasion. They do try their best and generally we get on well, but sometimes they can be so obtuse about things that to me seem simple to understand.

My humans' names are Sheila and Peter and I have lived with them since I was six weeks old when they collected me, together with my friend Tansy, from a refuge centre where we had been taken. I can't remember my kittenhood prior to that time and I feel it was probably quite traumatic so I have never tried to relive it.

Tansy and I were picked by Sheila and Peter, I've always assumed, because we stood out as the best looking of the bunch. I have an immaculate tabby coat in variegated stripes of co-ordinating shades of browns and tans and I can say that, even now that I admit to middle age starting to creep on, my coat is as thick and glossy as ever. Tansy, on the other hand, wore a rather ordinary catsuit in black and white longish fur, but in my opinion it was rather sparse. Still, she had a very cute little face and I suppose that's what attracted Sheila and Peter to her as well as me.

At first, and indeed for about fourteen years or so, we lived in a house with a very large garden, and even a woodland lake, in the heart of Cornwall. It was a paradise for cats. Apart from Tansy and yours truly we also had three other feline pals living with us - Lucky, a rather nice boy in a pale shade of ginger and white and Taro, a rather snooty aristocat, who claimed famous ancestors, and he did, I must admit, have rather unusually soft fur in trendy shades of cream and seal colour. Tansy and I often rather envied him his haute couture coat when the new season's feline fashions came out. Last but not least, there was dear Robbie, another ginger and white boy who, sadly, had only one eye.

We all got on moderately well, though Lucky was always my favourite and if he asked me nicely I did allow him to share my basket and keep my back warm. He always had rather a crush on me which was flattering, and I was not averse to the odd edible gifts he would bring me. He may have had thoughts at one time of even daring to propose, but I soon steered him off that track as both Tansy and I had become celibate right from our time in the refuge. Still, it was nice to have his adoration and I used to notice that Robbie and even snooty Taro watched me with a certain amount of longing (you can tell you know) whereas they both treated Tansy as a naughty younger-sister kitten.

♡
♡

Lucky, my hero!

4

We had quite a houseful in those days as, apart from we five cats of all different shapes, sizes and colours, we also had to endure two other major irritations! One was a large St Bernard dog called Hennessy who was for ever loping around and shaking off his fur all over us and drooling over our heads when he felt affectionate. The other was the sound of a large, foul-mouthed blue and yellow Macaw called Geronimo who made our eardrums rattle with his screeching. To complete the menagerie, there were tropical fish in a glass tank indoors and outdoor fish in the pond. The indoor variety seemed unreal to we cats, but we did have a bit of fun stalking and frightening the ones in the pond.

Now, sadly, all my old pussy companions are gone, and I even shed a tear when the slobbery old dog went to that big kennel in the sky, but I must admit I wasn't too sad when that wretched Macaw moved on to a place full of other Macaws and screeching parrots - how absolutely ghastly that place sounds!

So the humans and I have now moved to another house in a different part of Cornwall. I must admit I do like it here and of course I am now the sole kingpin - or should I say queenpin - in the new house, and I make quite sure that my carers never neglect their duties as far as my welfare is concerned. I like to think they enjoy looking after my diet, coiffure and litter tray, and I expect - and get - lots of pampering too. I am satisfied that they know my rules by now.

I make sure I take good care of myself by getting plenty of sleep and only eating healthy, life prolonging food. I never exert myself more than is absolutely necessary (why keep servants and do things yourself?) and I do make sure I test their patience from time to time - you must keep humans up to the mark at all times!

Anyhow, now you know something of how I came to be here

today so I hope you will find some pleasure in reading my diary for the week. It may even inspire you to keep one yourselves.

My Week -
Early Summer 2004

Sunday:

8.30am Was awakened from a rather nice dream - I was chasing a mother mouse and her three babies - by Peter stumbling down into the kitchen where I sleep. At least I do get a lie-in on Sundays as normally he rudely awakens me at the unearthly hour of 6.30am on weekdays - something about going out to earn money, whatever that is.

8.35am Found myself propelled towards the back door, my personal cat flap opened, and before I knew it I was through it and standing out on some dewy grass. He always does this to me - I tell you, would you like to take off your fur-lined knicks in wet grass early in the morning? Of course not!

8.36am I came back in.

8.37am Went on cat litter and performed. I like to see Peter's face when I do this. I particularly took the time to scuff up the litter so that quite a lot fell over the sides of the litter tray and onto the carpet. Then I sat and watched as he brushed it up into a dustpan and then made the top of the cat litter nice and clean and flat again. He was muttering a few words under his breath that I normally wouldn't like to hear in public, but when he glanced at me I gave him an encouraging nod and he got on with it and it was soon cleaned to my exacting standards once more. I don't know why he always 'kicks' against doing this particular little task - it is, after all, quite clearly detailed in his job description.

8.50am Now it was time for my weekly appointment with the furdresser. (This, again, is another 'hat' Peter wears.) He is quite good at styling my fur. Of course he's done it for years and he knows exactly how I like it. I've never been able to do my own fur - Tansy, if I recall, used to do hers quite stylishly, generally with a few carelessly placed knots in it, but Peter always then came along and undid all her handiwork. At this time of year I always shed a lot of excess fur and this, too, doesn't always go down well with the carers - they seem to take it as a personal affront if it settles on the sofa and Sheila sometimes utters those same words I heard Peter say earlier if she finds some of my fur on her skirt. I can't think why. I would have thought they would have been pleased to have gained some nice fur - after all, they don't seem to have any themselves. Well, my fur coiffing went quite well so I had no need to scratch Peter this week.

9.15am Decided to have some breakfast. I wish I could choose my own food. Generally I like what they give me, but if I eat a meal up quite quickly they keep repeating that menu as they think I really love it. Not true - I like variety and trying new tastes. I now tend to eat a little at a time and make the plate last most of the day until refill time. However, no food is wasted in this household - there is an eager mouth ready to devour everything I leave (more of that later!) Today the breakfast was prawn terrine with a lobster sauce - quite lip- smacking really!

10.00am Moved over into the dining room where I have a rather nice rug laid out in front of the patio doors which gets every bit of sun going. A lovely spot to relax in. After a leisurely wash and brush up to get rid of the lobster smell from my whiskers, I settled down for my morning sleep ...

12.30pm Something awoke me. It was the carers going out.

They quite often meet friends for lunch on a Sunday. Trouble is, they also quite often bring them back and disturb me. Oh well. I settled down again to make the most of the peace and quiet.

3.00pm Time to wake up and have a stroll around the garden. The cat flap was open so no problems there. As I climbed through it, the bell on my collar tinkled and I thought, "Oh dear, that'll bring my next-door neighbour round". He, too, worships the ground I walk on and can be a right pain at times. I sometimes wish I didn't have the wretched bell on my collar and the rather naff name tag with Truffles engraved on it; they make such a racket clinking together. This all stems back to when I was young and had a bit of a reputation for chasing little things in the garden of the old house - so a collar and bell were clamped round my neck and have been there ever since! I think the humans thought that it would warn away my prey, but little did they know it didn't stop me that often! Now, I'm afraid I'm just a bird watcher, not a catcher. As I've mentioned the collar, I will tell you, reader, that it is a nice designer collar bought specially in Florida with the exact matching tabby design of my coat. Anyway, I digress ...

3.03pm As I thought, Pandy the cat from next door came limping along to see me. He is quite a smart looking cat who wears a smooth-furred black and white catsuit and I must say he does keep himself extremely clean and his claws nice and short. I suppose I ought to feel a bit sorry for him really - he turned up out of the blue to adopt his owners who live next door (though this happened when they were in their previous house) having been living rough following some kind of road accident that left him with a permanent limp on one of his back legs. The family took him in together with their other two cats, Bob and Ty - more of them later. They then moved next door to us at nearly the same time as we moved here ourselves - about eighteen months ago. However, several months ago now they acquired a real little hooligan of a dog, a Westie puppy called Oscar, and Oscar has really put Pandy's nose out of joint as he is so boisterous. Consequently, Pandy spends most of his time trying to move in with us. I am certainly NOT having that - no way! If I feel that Peter and Sheila are weakening, I quickly give Pandy several fierce growls and spits in their earshot to ensure that they are quite certain we would not mix together! I am used to getting their undivided attention and no way will I share that!

3.10pm I sat on the patio in the sun keeping one eye on Pandy who was trying to creep nearer to me each minute. I let him get to within four patio slabs, then let him have it - spits, growls and hisses - the full lot. I love doing that. It makes me feel powerful. He is really quite frightened of me when I am in this kind of mood. Sometimes, though, if I want to tantalise him, but feel a little more kindly towards him, I'll keep my mouth shut - but he still doesn't dare come past the four patio slab boundary. He's a bit of a wimp really, prat I think your human expression is, but there again we must make allowances for his disability. Not for him, I suppose, the thrill of the chase with a mouse or a bird, and, although he can somehow haul himself up and over our neighbouring walls, he can't manage to negotiate my cat flap. That, of course, is a bonus knowing that he can't catch me. On the odd occasion he has tried his luck and attempted to chase me or pounce on me out of devilment, but I have always just dashed in through the cat flap which has slammed with a satisfactory bang behind me, stopping him in his tracks. I must say that even now I can still put on a turn of speed when necessary. Comes from my careful eating and looking after myself, I expect.

Pandy trespassing on my patio

4.30pm Pandy and I were still lounging around on the patio when I heard the humans, plus their friends, coming back. Pandy hobbled off somewhere and I nipped in via the kitchen to the upstairs study where I have my own chair from where I like to survey things and see who is visiting and what their credentials are before I decide whether to acknowledge them or not.

6.30pm Well, I must have nodded off - surprise, surprise!

6.45pm Had a nice stretch and a brief scratch and then walked downstairs to see who were the visitors that day. I hoped they wouldn't be staying too long in case it delayed my dinner time. Two humans I didn't recognise were sitting on the patio with mine, and they were all sipping Pimms (a most peculiar summer drink that humans seem to drink when it's hot; certainly not something I would like to pass my lips - give me nice fresh milk any time!) I kept an eye on them but avoided physical contact - ugh, nothing worse than fat, sweaty fingers running through my neatly brushed fur! My people think I am shy when they have visitors because I usually hide away and watch from a distance, but I'm not shy. I just don't like physical contact from strangers. Maybe I'm too fussy - lots of cats I know just love being stroked by any old Tom, Dick or Harry - but I prefer to get my pats from family and very close friends only. You know where they've been.

7.30pm Oops - I was dozing again. The people were leaving and generally milling around. I tried to get into the front hall and out of the front door undetected (one of my aims in life, as yet unfulfilled) but as usual they'd shut the door from the main hall so there was no chance! However, in the kitchen I saw that my dinner plate was full so I settled down to a nice meal. It was salmon and trout supreme this time; not bad - I do rather have a preference for fish dishes.

7.45pm Well, that wasn't bad - it filled a gap! Time for a last inspection of the garden. As I went out of the cat flap I noticed Pandy curled up under a chair staring at me in that besotted way he has. I took no notice and once I had done what I had intended to do in my favourite place at the back of the flower bed, I came right back inside leaving him out there - best place for him really! Oh dear, that does sound rather churlish doesn't it? I must try to be kinder to him - he is not so fortunate as I am.

8.00-11.15pm Dozed on Sheila's knees while she and Peter stared unblinkingly at a box in the corner of the lounge. Well, I say "they" but he very soon seemed to relax into a more horizontal position and fell asleep whilst making revolting snoring sounds. How inconsiderate can you be? I never admit to snoring! Ladylike purring is what I do! I don't see why they enjoy this strange pastime of staring into a corner, but they spend hours each evening in this position. They are looking at a large rectangular silver-coloured box with peculiar pictures coming and going on the face of it accompanied by various odd noises. It baffles me! Occasionally I have noticed images of birds flying on it and this, I must say, makes it all seem even more odd, but this may be a pure figment of my imagination. Oh well, each to their own as they say - I will never understand the human mind and certainly they will never understand mine!

11.20pm Bedtime. Back to the kitchen again. My night bed was put out for me (in the daytime I have a rather trendy leopard-skin print bed) and I flopped onto it. The end of a pleasant day ...

Monday:

6.40am My usual wake-up call from Peter. Why he seems obsessed with getting up halfway through the night I'll never know. Perhaps he doesn't sleep well. He should try counting fleas - that is always guaranteed to send cats to sleep. Might I say, however, that I do not harbour any fleas on my person. The humans apply some kind of drops to my neck about once every six weeks and since they've been doing this rather strange practice I've never seen one of the nasty little creatures (fleas, I mean, not humans!) My vet recommended these miracle drops. He is a nice man and always admires me and says how well I look for my age. I say flattery will get you everywhere and so I let him give me my annual injections and worming pill with no problems. If my humans have ever attempted to give me a worming pill, well that's a different story. I make it as difficult as possible for them - letting them think I have it safely in my mouth and then spitting it out! I can play that game for ages and sometimes they have actually given up. So that's definitely been one-up to me. Touch wood, I have never had to have any treatment for illnesses so far - poor Tansy was always at the vet's surgery having to have pills and potions forced upon her.

6.45am I stretched and started to uncurl from my nice soft bed. Pity to have to leave it! Peter was busily valeting my toilet area and renewing the litter. Each time I use it I try to see how far I can send a pawful of litter granules flying - my record so far has been about two metres. Usually he misses some pieces and so I have the satisfaction of seeing Sheila, when she comes down later, also having to bend down and pick up the odd bit! Childish (kittenish) I suppose I am sometimes ...

7.ooam It was a really bright, sunny morning so I didn't mind going out into the garden so early for a walkabout. The grass was quite dry and I didn't get nasty mud and grassy bits on my paws. Pandy was nowhere to be seen. However, a flash of long black and white fur from behind a rose bush told me that one of the other cats from next door, Bob, was on the scene. I am not too sure about Bob. He is young and in my opinion a typical hooligan who is too full of himself and is always trying his luck - needless to say, he gets short shrift from me. A hiss and a bunch of fives on his nose puts him in his place! I have caught him on several occasions peering at me whilst I have been performing private, personal functions on the back flower bed. A real little peeping Tom! Most off-putting really. He needs to find another young lady cat more his own age. I did hear the humans discussing him one day and they were saying that he is a bit of a devil -may-care type and likes winding up some of the other cats in the neighbourhood. For pure mischief he likes starting arguments amongst them in the hope that they will escalate into proper catfights. Actual fights rarely happen because after a lot of hissing and growling usually one of the cats will eventually lose interest and wander off. Sheila and Peter have a soft spot for Bob because he is the spitting image of Tansy. The first time I saw him walking along the top of our wall I must admit a shadow went over my heart too as I also, for a moment, thought it was Tansy resurrected!

7.20am Time for breakfast. Not a particularly appetising one this morning - some cheap cat crunchies they had acquired as a bargain buy and some leftovers from last night - so I didn't touch it and retired back to bed for another doze.

7.22-8.45am Slept.

8.50am Sheila arrived in the kitchen and as I had heard her coming, I was up and ready to greet her. We have quite lengthy conversations, though neither of us is quite sure what the other is trying to say. She is utterly hopeless at understanding even the basic words of cat language, though she makes a good attempt at imitating the sounds I make. All that does, though, is merely repeat everything I am trying to tell her in the first place! I was saying that Peter's idea of breakfast today was not mine, but all she seemed to be asking was what was wrong with it, why hadn't I eaten it, etc. Well, I couldn't be bothered to try any more to make her understand that in no way was I going to eat it, so I just walked away. Frustrating really.

11.30am I had been in the dining room in my sunny spot for a couple of hours or so when I saw Pandy come onto the patio. He ingratiates himself with the humans and is always asking for food, so I thought it was a pretty good bet that my unwanted breakfast would go his way. Sure enough I saw Sheila put the plate out and he polished off the contents in seconds. He gives them the wrong impression that he is poor and hard done by and they take it all in, silly humans. I know he is rather a sad character and I must try to be more tolerant of him and be nicer to him, but with regard to his winkling food out of people, I take my hat off to him as he has it down to a fine art! Peter is his main target. Pandy knows what time Peter leaves the house in the morning and also roughly what time he returns. He knows that he drives up in his motor machine and then opens the large flap at the front of the house in which the machine sleeps at night. Whilst Peter is opening this flap, Pandy limps as quickly as he can right into the space and hides under a second motor machine that also lives in there. He then refuses to budge until Peter fills a dish with food and waves it in front of him. In fact, what Pandy is given is my leftovers - as you know, it is bad manners to eat everything off your plate so I always leave a little something from every meal. Sheila collects these remnants up and puts them by for Pandy. He, of course, thinks the food is prepared especially for him, but oh no, it's only what I decide to leave for him. Call it my contribution to charity if you like - who am I to spoil his illusion? Anyway, Pandy's little scheme works like clockwork. Peter tempts him around the back of the house with the dish, and Pandy eats the food while Peter houses the motor machine. Everyone is happy. Sometimes Pandy chances his luck and manages to get two portions of food. If he eats quickly enough and can get back around before Peter has managed to drive the machine into its space, he then nips in again and the whole saga is repeated! Grudgingly I give Pandy top marks for this scam of his.

This is a great drive-in cat cafe!

1.30pm Well, where does the time go? I must have dropped off again. It is so warm and pleasant in this room.

1.45pm I strolled into the kitchen. Sheila was sitting at the table having her lunch. I knew that if I sat right by her and stared fixedly up at her she would give me some titbits from her meal, though initially she would tell me that she wouldn't give me anything. I knew better - the fixed stare always works and she relents in the end. Today it was a Scotch egg - delicious! Certainly a hundred times better than my bog-standard breakfast offering. I wonder why human meals always smell better than cat meals? And why, even if you have a full dish yourself, the food on their plates always looks much better? I suppose it's a case of "the grass is always greener on the other side of the fence". That was a case in point, literally, a few years ago in our other house. I will remove myself to the patio now and when I am comfortable I'll tell you the story.

1.50pm On the patio now. You remember I mentioned that one of my companions in those days was snooty Taro, the aristocat, pedigree Birman cat. Well, even he wasn't so above us all that he wouldn't stoop to some cat burglary! On two occasions he carried off quite spectacular coups. Once, we were all in the garden and as it was a hot, sunny day our next-door neighbour was also sitting in hers. Our humans were eating sandwiches but the neighbour had a nicely prepared pilchard salad accompanied by a bottle of that coloured liquid humans like to drink. All was beautifully set out on the table on a nice cloth with a napkin etc. She always liked to have things just so ... Well, suddenly her little machine - through which somehow humans mysteriously speak to their friends - made a loud ringing noise so she went indoors to answer it. She was only gone for less than a minute or two. However, Taro, who had been on the lookout ever since he smelt the lovely odour of pilchards, immediately took his chance, leapt onto the table and deftly removed the pilchards, leaving the salad leaves intact. He was gone in a flash. A truly masterful move and one I have remembered with admiration to this day! When the neighbour returned to the table, for a moment she didn't realise that anything was different. Then something clicked - her pilchards had disappeared! Of course we never said anything, and when a day or so later she mentioned what had happened to Sheila and Peter they never had the bottle to tell her the truth either! The other occasion when Taro carried out a masterly theft involved a Scotch egg! Funny - humans must like these eggs as much as cats do, though what kind of bird lays such crispy-coated eggs I shudder to think. They must get very sore bottoms! However, I'll tell you that story later - I'm feeling tired again now.

5.45pm Goodness me - what happened to the past four hours or so? Part of my sleep programme of course! You humans should know that cats try to sleep for up to twenty-two hours out of twenty-four. That's why in cat years we live comparatively longer than you do - we conserve far more energy!

5.50pm I wondered if anything had been put into my dinner bowl (nobody had called me) so I decided to investigate in the kitchen. As I approached, a nauseous smell came wafting through the air and I could see some saucepans on the hob boiling away with clouds of white stuff going up into the air. I recognised the smell - curry I've heard them call it - so I knew the humans were going to be eating an Indian meal this evening. I can never understand why they want to eat foreign stuff. A good plain dish of meat or fish is quite sufficient and far more healthy in my opinion. I did once sample some Bombay duck. Now I am not averse to a nice bit of tasty duck and so I thought that I would enjoy tasting the Indian version. I nibbled it eagerly but, oh dear, oh dear, it was totally awful! Nothing at all like our own meaty British duck-tasting ducks - it was all dry and fishy! I spat it out - ugh!

6.15pm I had been sitting in my bed, my whiskers crinkling with the horrible smell of the curry, when suddenly a horrific high-pitched wailing sound made my fur stand on end and I jumped out of the bed, in my haste toppling over a three-tiered rack which stands beside it filled with strange orange, red and lemon round-shaped objects. I've often wondered what these peculiar objects are that the humans eat - they have a sickly sweet smell that I find very unappetising. Anyway, these objects decanted themselves all over the floor. Sheila was saying those words she shouldn't and then Peter appeared and started to get over excited, I thought, waving his arms about and shouting. However, he reached up to a point by the ceiling above the door and thank goodness the awful sound stopped. He very nearly fell over the debris on the floor - I rather wish he had, I like seeing how clumsy humans are. You would never see a cat trip over anything - we are much too sure-footed. However, Sheila calmed him down and soon the floor was clear, the saucepans were emptied onto their plates, the steam subsided and thankfully the smell did too. My bowl appeared with some nice chicken in it and we all began to eat. Peace reigned.

7.15-11.00pm Slept fitfully on Sheila's knees while they stared incessantly as usual at the silver box in the corner of the lounge. My nerves were still jangling from the upset in the kitchen earlier and that ghastly siren going off. (I think I heard Peter call it a smoke alarm, though he added an adjective beginning with 'b' in front of it!) The whole thing was really quite frightening for someone of my temperament and should not have happened. I expect to live in a quiet and well-ordered environment. Usually it is, but occasionally, like this evening, the humans trip up. Talking of tripping up reminds me of rather a funny incident that I had a hand in a few years ago. I think I mentioned earlier that from time to time we cats like to try the patience of humans - it keeps them up to scratch (pardon the pun!) When the gang of us - Lucky, Tansy, Taro, Robbie and myself - were all living together, one or other of us liked to hide when we were called in for the evening curfew. This would always infuriate the humans who would spend a needless half hour or more repeatedly walking around the garden calling the name of the missing cat. This game was more enjoyable when it was raining. Eventually the cat would be found sitting on the doorstep. Lucky was the past master at this game. We prided ourselves that not once did the humans ever realise that our hiding places were right nearby! They never spotted us. Really they were so unobservant; they had totally no idea - no self-respecting cat would ever lose sight of its prey. Anyway, Peter was shouting for me one evening and after about three-quarters of an hour I decided to make myself seen. He came rushing out and tried to grab me as I stood near, but not right by, the doorway. As he attempted to pick me up I neatly side-stepped, but he, carrying on moving through the momentum of his run, tripped over and fell right into the centre of a large, low flowering shrub growing by the edge of the house. Leaves and petals scattered everywhere - I also scattered! But I couldn't contain my laughter as he was totally stuck and had to be hauled up by Sheila who, I was glad to see, was also choking with suppressed laughter. To be on the safe side, I did keep out of his way for a few days and I was truly sorry that he hurt his knee, but I still chuckle about the incident even now. It was definitely another one-up to me!

11.10pm Retired to bed.

Tuesday:

6.35am Another unearthly wake-up call. I did not feel in the least like getting up this morning and refused to budge when Peter wanted to try his usual trick of bunging me out through the cat flap. I think he must have some kind of perverted sense of humour in seeing me tip-pawing through the wet morning grass. Anyway, it didn't work today.

7.45am As soon as I heard him leaving the house I got up and made my own way through the cat flap. By this time the bright sunlight had dried up the grass so it was no hardship walking over it. There was no point in using my litter tray as I wouldn't have the pleasure of watching him collect up the granules, so I performed my morning ablutions and toilet in my private spot at the back of the garden. Even that loutish Bob wasn't around to spy on me and I felt rather content with my lot and at peace with myself. I sat and just drank in the nice sunlight for ten minutes or so and then returned to have my breakfast before Sheila appeared on the scene.

10.30am I dozed in the sun. It being such a lovely day, Sheila was avoiding her duties and she spent most of the day sitting on the patio leafing through various celebrity magazines, though I knew when Peter returned home she would tell him how busy she had been doing housework all day! I told you that she and I have a good rapport so I would never give her away, but as you know, dear reader, cats are always very crafty so I could probably somehow contrive to spill the beans on her if she ever really upset me!

1.30pm Lunch in the garden. Very nice. Sheila had some ham sandwiches and I enjoyed some off cuts of the ham. I must say that she is a soft touch when it comes to giving titbits. Although my own food is generally very acceptable, as ever, humans' food seems so much tastier. I especially like that rather odd stuff they call cheese. Now, I have heard of a Cheshire cat, but I was unaware that there is also a Cheshire cheese - and very nice it is too!

2.15pm Whilst we were still lazing on the patio, Pandy arrived, though he took care not to position himself too close to me. In some ways I wish he did have a little more 'oomph' but I think he's never forgotten how I growled and spat at him when he first ventured into my space. I wouldn't really do anything nasty to him, but he must be kept in his place. I think I may have a 'Be nice to Pandy day' tomorrow. That will surprise him! I may even let him get to within just two patio slabs away from me. He will then be able to admire me from quite close - the lucky lad! I have noticed that recently he has taken a chance and entered our kitchen through the back door when Sheila's left it open. (As I said before, if it's closed he can't make it through the cat flap because of his bad leg.) If I've been sitting inside the kitchen when he's got in, one fixed stare from me and he's backed out again. Once or twice, though, he's got in when I've been in the garden. He has at least had the nerve to explore a bit and once even found time apparently to have a kip as Sheila found incriminating black and white hairs on one of their beds! So I respect Pandy for proving that even he can be crafty when he wants to be - and, of course, the daily food scam with Peter proves that!

Mmmm, these lovely warm chippings ...

4.00pm I took a stroll round the garden. There is a nice little flower bed in the centre where the plants are embedded in slate chippings. In the sun these warm up nicely and are rather delightful to lie on. So, after the ritual of flexing my front claws on the log surround to this bed, I flopped onto it and made myself lovely and comfortable with the sun still pouring down. Throughout the garden there are lots of statues of we cats - a way the humans have of showing just how much they worship us. I must say it is a nice feeling to be adored and, credit where credit's due, I havn't had much to complain about with Peter and Sheila as they've looked after my every whim. They have tried hard to meet my exacting standards and, if I am honest, I couldn't have found a better human family, but don't tell them that as it will make them swollen headed! Dear me, I am getting very sentimental now, it must be the sun relaxing me! So ... time to have a nap once more.

6.15pm I headed back to the kitchen. With a bit of miaow talk I managed to get Sheila to understand that my supper was needed promptly. All that sun had made me feel rather peckish. In Sheila's case, all that sun had made her feel rather lethargic. Anyway, she eventually understood and a full dish was put on the mat; something I like very much today - mackerel in jelly. Peter and Sheila also had a fish meal - nothing like fish to keep you healthy I say - but Peter had to collect theirs from the fish and chip shop in the village. Sheila's lazy day was still continuing.

6.45-8.45pm No silver box this evening - they sat in the garden with me. All in all it was very pleasant. The birdsong sounded lovely, the evening sun still shone and all was quiet and peaceful. What more could a cat want?

11.10pm Well, another day over - a day full of nothing really but somehow I felt even more tired at the end of it than usual. I looked forward to a good night's rest and hoped it wouldn't be too hot. The one snag with wearing a fur catsuit is that you can't unzip it when you want to. Humans' outer coverings seem to come undone and can be removed if they get too hot - that is about the only advantage they have over we cats!

Wednesday:

6.40am Well, the weather was still lovely so I didn't mind getting up so early and I went through the cat flap before Peter even tried to persuade me - that must have surprised him! I am going to have a 'Be nice to Pandy day' today so I might as well be nice to Peter too.

7.00am Ablutions all done, I sat savouring the sunshine and the fresh smells in the garden. Pandy dropped down over the neighbouring wall and crept slowly towards me expecting my usual greeting hiss, but I kept my mouth shut and even managed a small version of a Cheshire cat grin. Pandy lay down not too far away and put on his adoring look. I preened myself and licked my paws whilst keeping an eye on him - yes, I suppose it is nice to have an admirer. I have had a few in my time - I've always been pretty choosy with whom I associate, though you don't always have to have a posh upbringing to be attractive. Lucky was the one, I suppose, that I liked the best - he was flamboyant in a ginger sort of way and always had a devil-may-care attitude. He was a farm kitten that my humans had rescued when he had been hit by one of those infernal motor machines. He was only about three months old at the time and was lucky (hence his name!) that they came along at the time as he was lying in the road concussed with a fractured lower jaw. Nasty. Anyway, after a visit to the vet's he was soon made fit and well and came into their home. At the time I was not on the scene, but when Tansy and I were adopted a couple of years later, Lucky was very good to us, showing us the ropes - like where the local vole and mice nests were situated (he was a great hunter, having had to fend for himself right from his rather inauspicious start in the farmyard) and where the best sunny spots were in the garden. He always had interesting tales to tell, including how he came to be adopted after his accident. But it was Pandy's day today, so I removed thoughts of Lucky from my mind and carried on smiling at Pandy, but he very soon sloped off somewhere.

8.00am I came in for breakfast and then strolled into the dining room to spend the next few hours on my sunny mat. I could see Pandy outside on the patio. He came and looked through the glass at me. Usually I give a growl and flatten my ears when he does this, but today I merely smiled. This seemed to unnerve him even more than when I growl! He curled up a few feet away and we both prepared for our morning slumber period. Whilst I was in dozing mode I pondered over his rather odd name. Why 'Pandy'? I asked myself. Could it be short for Andy Pandy, some sort of puppet I'd heard Sheila talk about when they first knew Pandy's name. But Andy Pandy used to wear a blue and white suit; Pandy's is black and white. Well, sleep was coming - I couldn't be bothered to wonder about it any more ...

12.30pm Well, doesn't time fly - snack time again. I didn't feel particularly hungry so I just picked at a few crunchies that were in my bowl. Sheila wasn't in today. Wednesday is her day for going into town, so I have the house to myself. She thinks I sleep all day on my mat. Silly human! Doesn't she know that humans' beds are just irresistible to a cat? I have long been accustomed to a Wednesday afternoon nap on their bed, but as I have always covered my tracks very carefully, they've never noticed. The tip is to resist having a scratch or a lick and brush up whilst on the bed as that leaves traces of fur.

1.00pm Today I didn't have a sleep on the bed - the sun was so lovely that I went outside to join Pandy. By this time he was lying on the warm slate chippings on the flower bed, so I made myself comfortable on the opposite side of the flower bed. We remained in this companionable state until Sheila arrived home at about three. I think she was genuinely pleased that I had let Pandy spend the afternoon with me. I do think in a way that Pandy should get out more - I know that I have this fatal attraction for him but he is not very old and surely there must be more exciting things for him to do than lie around with me. Still, I mustn't forget that his leg prohibits him from any real chases, hunting etc.

4.30pm Still sleepy, but I was in a reminiscing mood. When I was a bright young thing I was always out and about hunting or stalking, but nowadays I just prefer to snooze and remember. One incident that stands out in my mind is one that the humans often tell their friends about. It inevitably brings a laugh! The joke of the story is on me but I don't really mind - it even makes me smile still! It was a lovely sunny day, like today, when we were all living in the previous house. Sheila was sitting on the patio sunning herself - pity she goes such a nasty red colour. I bet she wishes her coat was in beautiful shades of brown and tan like mine! The big slobbery dog, Hennessy, was beside her, tongue lolling out, trying to keep in the shade, and Tansy was there as well, basking in the sun and sound asleep. I was under the conifer hedge nearby, resting after quite an agreeable morning when I had caught a reasonably large slow worm, and now there, just in front of me, was a tasty-looking fat mouse. Perhaps the mouse was feeling the heat too, because it was sitting dozing and foolishly not looking over its shoulder - when it would immediately have seen me! Dear me, the number of mice and voles I used to catch mostly because they weren't following the small mammals' safety code, which states that they should continually be on the alert for predators 24/7. Anyway, although I wasn't feeling particularly hungry, this target was too good to miss! I sprang into action. The mouse gave a startled squeak, but too late - I had already got it by the scruff of the neck. It's piercing squeak, however, had alerted the group on the patio. Sheila has always had a penchant for trying to rescue the creatures that we cats like to catch and she jumped up, saw me with the mouse, shouted, and started to chase me. Well, I like a good chase! We made quite a funny sight I should think, charging round the conifer hedge - me first, with the mouse still squeaking at the top of its voice, Sheila trying to catch me up, and Hennessy lumbering along behind. And Tansy slept through it all! After a couple of turns round the hedge, I arrived back at the patio and paused under the table, making sure that I had the mouse in a firm grip. Sheila and Hennessy ranged themselves opposite me. Then Sheila played a sneaky trick - she threw something to my right and, as I momentarily turned to see what it was, the mouse took its chance and escaped from my grasp. But then things happened so quickly that I was simply astounded and all I could do was gasp! The mouse made its bid for freedom, and leapt forward but in doing so it literally jumped straight at Hennessy - who had his enormous mouth open - and disappeared right down his throat! I remained frozen and gobsmacked! Sheila lunged at Hennessy and, putting her hands around his neck, tried to retrieve the mouse, but no, like Jonah and the whale, the mouse had well and truly gone! I really don't know who was the most surprised - me, Hennessy or Sheila! Tansy, amazingly, was still asleep. Anyway, I did hear that Sheila followed Hennessy around for the rest of the day but no trace of the mouse was ever found. Pity really, nobody was a winner and the mouse was certainly a loser!

The disappearing mouse illusion - not appreciated by me!

7.30pm Well, dinner was not particularly memorable but in this hot spell nobody was really hungry. The humans sat around in the garden after their own dinner and nobody said much. We were all savouring the hot spell and relaxing. Well, I relax most of the time anyway - as I said before, we cats never get stressed and wound up like humans seem to do. We have got the right idea about life - sleep, eat good food regularly, do as little as possible, and make sure you have your human carers willing and well trained. What more can a cat want?

11.00pm Bed.

Thursday:

6.30am The dreaded morning wake-up call from Peter. I do dislike being disturbed so early, but because he seems to enjoy seeing the delights of the dawning of each new day he assumes that I do as well. He wasn't quite so cheerful this time, though, as I had been up a couple of times in the night with a queasy tummy

- don't know why as I didn't have much to eat yesterday with it being so hot - and I hadn't quite been able to make it to the litter tray! He was mumbling those unnecessary words again as he shoved me through the cat flap. No point going out now, I thought, as the deed had already been done, but to keep him happy I wandered around outside for about ten minutes thinking this would give him time to clean up around my toilet area. After yesterday, this morning was pretty dull, chilly and dismal. The grass was wet and horrid sticky drops of moisture were falling off the leaves of plants as I brushed by. This made my fur wet and spiky and did not put me in the best of humour. Consequently, when I came back indoors I went straight back to bed and, ignoring Peter, curled up and went to sleep again.

8.45am Woke up, stretched and went to inspect the litter tray. Yes, he'd done the cleaning job nicely, though a sickly sweet scent of flowers prevailed all around the area. The humans have a nearby cupboard full of bottles of liquids and cans of revolting-smelling sprays which they seem to think smell better than the natural catty odours I would prefer around my corner. Pity they don't get spray cans perfumed with fishy or poultry smells, which would be so much nicer.

9.00am Inspected my dish and found some rather tasty cheesy crunchies in it with bacon pieces. By this time I was feeling quite hungry, so I polished off breakfast in double-quick time. Feeling much more perky now I went outside to see if the sun was shining. Well, it was making an effort, darting in and out between the clouds which were scudding by at quite a rate. A fair breeze had got up so I found a sheltered spot by the wall and sat down to lick my whiskers and face clean after the bacon and cheese.

10.00am Pandy ambled by and sat down not too far away. But today was NOT a 'be nice to Pandy day' so I flattened my ears and growled warningly at him. He retreated to the other side of the garden table, nervously watching for my next move. Oh I must say I do rather like having this power over him! Anyway, we both sat quietly for quite a while, savouring the sun.

12.10pm A movement to my right caught my eye and it was Ty, another of the cats from next door. Ty and I have never really had much to do with each other. He occasionally passes through our garden to the one behind and we have only made the most cursory nods to each other. I know that Pandy doesn't get on too well with him or the other scallywag, Bob. I think that they are both a bit scornful of Pandy's disability and he, in turn, prefers to keep the peace and keep out of their way. Ty was carrying something in his mouth - a bird I think - but he soon disappeared through the hedge. I compared Ty to Lucky. Lucky was a champion hunter, as I think I mentioned previously, and was a really feisty character afraid of nothing and nobody. Ty seems to me to be of the same ilk. I have heard at times the sound of him and/or Bob squaring up to some of the other cats in this neighbourhood. Lucky had quite a few fights in his time and never chickened out whatever the size or tenacity of his opponents! One in particular, I remember was an extremely large, long-furred coal-black tom who moved into the area and immediately began terrorising the local cats, particularly the females. An abnormal amount of black kittens soon appeared in the neighbourhood and I used to hear our humans talking about this and the black cat whose human carers didn't appear to restrict him in any way. People nicknamed him Saddam. Lucky and Saddam had several skirmishes, one of which resulted in Lucky having to have a hasty visit to the vet and an operation to fix a scratch on his eye. One day, however, we heard one hell of a catfight going on outside. Sheila went out to find Lucky pinned against the garage wall by Saddam, both of them with paws striking out at each other. Trouble was that Saddam's front legs were a lot longer than Lucky's and Lucky's punches were all falling short. You human readers may equate the scene to imagining the boxers Frank Bruno versus Barry McGuigan in the same situation! Sheila's cries to break them up didn't work, but fortunately just then the postman turned up and, realising that the situation could have ended up pretty nastily for Lucky, he somehow managed to plunge in and grab Lucky away. Saddam ran off. Lucky, give him his due, was furious with the postman for extracting him from the fight which, of course, he insisted to me afterwards he would eventually have won. But even I thought that he was being over-optimistic on this occasion! Sheila gave the postman a cup of coffee, and I sat with Lucky and calmed him down. It was a long time before he forgot what he thought was the humiliation of being extracted from a fight, and after that he was for ever on the lookout for Saddam to get his revenge. However, if not to Lucky's, it was to the relief of the rest of us that a couple of months later Saddam disappeared from the scene. The humans thought that his owners had moved away. So that was the end of a chapter of terrorisation of the local felines by one evil cat.

Lucky and Saddam's big boxing match!

1.30pm Lunchtime. My appetite was certainly much better today and I had a delightful mixture this time of cod and haddock with a piquant cheesy sauce that just tripped off the tongue! Pandy was also given a dish of this and he scoffed it in about ten seconds flat. Obviously unused to gourmet food, he should have savoured each mouthful as I did - makes it seem to last longer too!

1.45pm After that meal I retired to the dining room window and prepared to spend the rest of the afternoon on the mat dozing in the sun.

6.00pm The humans had an old friend who'd arrived to stay for a few days and, whilst Sheila was in the kitchen fussing over their dinner, Peter and Lois, the friend, were having a drink in the sitting area of the dining room. I was lying beside them feeling at peace with the world with Lois stroking my fur. She is one of the few people I allow to touch me but, having known her all my life, and knowing that Sheila and her have been friends since they were kittens themselves, I trust her completely. For some reason Peter and Lois were talking about ghosts. At this point I must tell you that although the humans find it totally impossible to understand cat language, I can understand a lot of their words. They only think I know simple words like 'dinner', my name 'Truffles', 'stop it', 'no' or 'come in,' etc., but they would be surprised if they knew quite what I did understand, and they'd also be very nervous if I could actually talk in human language because I could spill lots of beans as they say! Because of the shape of a cat's mouth and throat and our type of larynx that isn't possible, so they can be relieved on that score! But I digress again ...

6.15pm Whilst Peter and Lois were talking about ghosts, suddenly we all jumped as from the chimney came ominous rustling and whirring sounds. I sprang up and they both stopped talking in mid-sentence and listened - more whirring noises sounding very ghostly! All of a sudden down the chimney fell a blackbird. My goodness, manna from heaven I thought! It flew to the patio doors, but as I began to run towards it Peter did a leap forward worthy of one of the best rugby players and grabbed the confused bird. He opened the door and it flew out. Well, what a swizz I thought - that would have made a nice snack for me. Oh well it was not to be. The story of my life I suppose - missed opportunities!

9.30pm Dinner for the humans finished and I was quite sated myself with the titbits Lois had passed to me under the table. They removed themselves to the lounge and started looking at the strange silver box again, only this time they seemed to be watching something from which I could swear I heard their own voices. Whatever it was they seemed to enjoy it and the conversation was all about their recent holiday. Their holidays are definitely not a thing I enjoy. I will tell you about that tomorrow probably - I'm feeling sleepy now.

12.10pm Finally to my proper bed. Activities went on in the kitchen for much longer than usual tonight, so I had no chance of any peace before the humans all, thankfully, disappeared to their own beds.

Friday:

6.30am Well, I slept much better than last night and never even had to disturb the litter tray, so I got a pat on the head and a big smile from Peter this morning. Smarmy devil being so patronising! Still, I must keep in his good books because it's my big day tomorrow and I hope he and Sheila will be giving me a nice treat! Silly aren't I, making a big thing of a birthday? Perhaps living with humans for so long is making me become humanised myself! Nooooh ... heaven forbid! That's the last thing I want to become. It's a cat's life for me! I went out into the garden and found it was another good day with plenty of sunshine already. Lovely. I examined the flower bed at the back of the garden, found a nice comfy spot and sat ... Bob ran past not even noticing me in his haste to get to the garden on the other side of us. The lady there puts out food for the birds each day on her lawn - nice bits and pieces of bread and pastry - and so Bob, who is rather greedy, always makes her garden his first port of call. I stretched after my efforts on the flower bed, filled in the hole I'd made - always neat and tidy, that's me - and strolled back to the kitchen.

6.45am Peter must have been in a good mood today as he spent more time than usual patting me and tickling me under the chin. Foolish, I know, but it really makes me feel good! I could sit and dream for hours with someone tickling me under the chin. Sheila quite often sits with me on her knee doing just that.

7.00am Ate breakfast and settled into the usual routine of whisker and face licking. In fact I had a good all-over wash whilst I was about it. We cats are very fastidious in our personal habits - even rather hippy, travelling cats out in the wilds will never neglect washing themselves. Another reason why we cats survive so well, as we don't let ourselves pick up diseases from being dirty. I moved on into the dining room to catch the warmth of the sun. Sheila and Lois joined me and ate their breakfast. I can't understand their need to use so many dishes for their meals. One bowl for food and one for water is surely quite sufficient. Another thing humans should learn from cats! Think of the washing-up time they'd save.

11.30am The humans have gone out for the day so once more I've been left to dream and reminisce in peace. This time, of course, they are only going out for the day. Sometimes they disappear for two or three weeks. Quite inconsiderate if you ask me. This is when they go on their holidays. As I mentioned yesterday, this is not a good time for cats. We do not expect our carers to leave their posts. They may well be going to enjoy themselves and get away from their normal day-to-day existence, but for them to do this means that we cats have to make a sacrifice. We are imprisoned in cat holiday camps. In my case I have to admit I go into a very nice, luxurious cattery quite near to where we used to live, but I will never let on to the humans that actually I don't really mind it too much. I let them think that I loathe it and I take quite a bit of pleasure in seeing that Peter, in particular, always gets terribly upset seeing me locked up. I draw on my full acting talents to ensure that he thinks I am suffering most dreadfully. Sometimes I've gone rather over the top and he's nearly cancelled the holiday at the last moment, but Sheila - being an astute female like me - knows that I am putting it on a bit so she's always persuaded him to grin and bear it. Him grin and bear it - I'm the one that's had to grin and bear it! When they take me there I am crammed into a horribly small wicker basket where I can barely turn round, sat on a blanket on top of newspaper, which I find extremely humiliating because it makes it look as if I am incontinent and can't last out for the three-quarters of an hour journey to the cattery. I really do not like going in this basket, which also takes me to the vet for my annual check-up. From the minute I am shut in the basket, therefore, I have always screamed at the top of my voice for the entire trip - non-stop. It does give me a bit of a sore throat but it also gives me a great satisfaction in knowing that I am annoying them intensely. Well, I do try to make them pay for the injustice of being locked in a basket. When we arrive at the cattery I am decanted into what is really quite a nice apartment facing a lawned square with trees and flowers. The apartment is on two levels. The ground floor has a nice-sized area for exercise, including a toilet corner and eating section. A handy tree trunk leads to the upper section where there is a proper house with windows and a door that I can get in and - this is the bit I really like - it has a heated floor! Really lovely to lie on, particularly in the winter months. At one end of the complex is a music machine and that is kept on all day long so we have something nice to listen to. I can see out of the apartment's upper floor to the fields and wood behind and can hear birdsong most of the time. So, as I said, as cat prisons go, this is a good one. The complex of apartments is always kept immaculate by a nice lady called Anne who I have got to know well over the years. I believe she looks forward to seeing me and she always takes time each day to pat me and have a chat whilst she is cleaning out. However, when I first arrive and go into the apartment, I still scream continually until Peter and Sheila leave. I like to think that on the way home they are feeling sorry for me and guilty that they have abandoned me. Of course, as soon as they are out of sight, Anne gives me some food and I settle myself down and make myself quite comfortable. It's really like being in a hotel - sit around all day, a bit of exercise if you feel like it climbing the tree trunk, and wait for the next meal to be served. Still, we are locked in and nobody has ever escaped from the complex to taste proper freedom. But, however nice they make it, there's just nothing like getting back home and feeling the freedom as you go out through your own cat flap!

1.15pm Woke up from a dreamless sleep, had a pleasant scratch and went into the kitchen. Beef on the menu for lunch today. Not bad.

1.30pm Went out through the cat flap to find Pandy already stretched out on the patio. He didn't stir when I approached, though he was watching my every move. I couldn't be bothered to growl or hiss so I laid down a few patio slabs away. With a full tummy after all that beef, sleep was ever drawing near again. So we both slept a couple of hours or so away ... I did tell you, it's a cat's life!

4.00pm Had a toilet break at the bottom of the garden. Pandy also woke up and vanished over the wall next door. Maybe some of the birds' titbits were left on the lawn! He is always ready to eat whatever is offered. I know that Sheila gives him my leftovers each evening, though I hadn't left much today. Funny how some cats are obsessed by food. Personally, I have never over-eaten, perhaps that is why my figure is as good as when I was a youngster. Taro the aristocat could also never turn down the unexpected, unusual titbit. This may have stemmed back to when he was a kitten. When he arrived at Sheila and Peter's home from his posh breeder, so he once told me, his breeder had sent a list of foods he was to be given. These included pilchards in tomato sauce, chicken breasts, scrambled eggs, fresh liver and cream, amongst the more everyday sorts of stuff. I told you the other day about Taro stealing our neighbour's pilchards, well here's the tale of when he nicked a Scotch egg with somewhat disastrous results. One day Sheila and Peter had been at home lunchtime and Sheila had put their meals on trays ready to eat outside. She took Peter's out, but when she returned to collect her own, the Scotch egg she had on her plate had vanished! Taro had neatly swiped it off the tray as soon as she had left the room! However, it was to prove his downfall because after taking only one bite from it he decided to run off with it and finish it at his leisure. He started to go down the stairs but Hennessy the big slobbery dog saw him with the Scotch egg and lunged out at it, somehow toppling Taro back down the last three stairs. Crack!! Taro's back leg fractured! My goodness, then there was consternation in the camp. Taro gave a shrill cry, dropped the Scotch egg and Hennessy grabbed it and was off. He did, I think, feel pretty mortified that he had caused Taro to injure himself. He always was a very clumsy dog. He did apologise to Taro afterwards but I don't think Taro ever forgave him. Anyway, this entailed an urgent visit to the vet for Taro who returned with his leg enveloped in a huge plaster and bandage which made the leg considerably longer than his other three! Seeing him get around was as if he was walking on a tripod, and for the first day or two he kept falling over sideways. He soon mastered the trick of it, though, and was speeding around pretty well as normal. We could always tell when he was coming down the stairs as we heard the bumpety-bump of the plastered leg coming down behind him! I am pleased to say that three weeks later the plaster was removed and his leg was as good as new. Taro kept out of Hennessy's way after that incident and I don't recall him ever stealing any more Scotch eggs!

Aaaah! Poor Taro ...

6.30pm All the humans had returned from their day out. Sheila and Lois had been visiting together with thousands of other humans in some kind of enormous garden under plastic domes - 'The Eden Project' they called it, but the only Eden I ever recall hearing about had only two people in it and a snake and an apple. Peter had returned from earning money - don't know why humans lay such store on getting money; cats get on very well without it.

9.00pm Well, all of us, human and feline, were sat down feeling full after our dinners. Pandy was with us outside in the garden and it was still pleasantly warm, the sun only just starting to dim a little. The humans chatted and we cats dozed. What's new?

11.30pm Bedtime again. How time rolls by - it hardly seems a day goes by before it's time to sleep again ...

Saturday:

8.30am Well, I was wide awake when Peter came down into the kitchen - after all, this was my big day! I was rewarded with an extra-long pat and caress from him and I then went outside and was pleased to see that the sun had put his hat on especially for me and all was bright and lovely in the garden. The sun shines on the blessed so they say, and in my case that's very true! I do feel blessed with a comfortable home and caring humans. Many cats struggle to survive in horrible circumstances or have to fend for themselves in a wide world populated with many very frightening things and uncaring humans, but, as I said, I am one of the lucky ones. I found a super family. But I mustn't get maudlin just because I've reached the milestone age of sixteen. I am only going to admit to just arriving towards old age - I feel I'm only in the departure lounge now, not out on the runway yet!

There are many more years in me to come! As I was carrying out my ablutions on the flower bed Bob and Ty strolled by, so for once I nodded and smiled at them and they, in turn, gave a couple of cheery miaows in return.

8.35am Back in the kitchen and Peter had brush in hand ready to style my fur for my special day. I had to look my best! Sheila then appeared and made a great fuss of me, kissing me (ugh!), and she excitedly produced an enormous birthday card for me (humans seem to have this habit of giving each other these cards, though it seems a bit silly to me as you can't eat a birthday card). Anyway it appeared to be a large picture of a tabby cat not unlike myself and they had obviously taken much trouble over choosing this card, so I pretended I was very pleased with it and purred loudly as they stood it near my breakfast bowl. However, I was more concerned that at the moment the bowl stood empty. I was not to be disappointed though as Sheila busied herself filling it up with crabmeat! Wow, my absolute favourite! I felt this was going to be a day to remember - it was certainly starting off well!

9.30am The humans and their friend Lois were seated at the dining room table having their breakfast and I was basking in the sun in my favourite spot. From their conversation it appeared that some more friends of theirs were due to arrive shortly, so it seemed that we would have a houseful to celebrate my birthday! Looking through the glass of the patio doors, I suddenly saw Pandy. He was clutching what looked like a bird in his mouth and indicating that I should come outside. I got up and ran out into the kitchen and through the cat flap. Pandy laid the bird at my feet. How very sweet of him to give me such a nice present on my birthday. A tear almost came into my eye, but I blinked it away. I mustn't let him know that underneath my sometimes prickly exterior I do have a big soft spot for him. I was amazed that he had even got hold of a bird as I would have thought he was unable to move quickly enough to catch anything. Whilst we were sitting there with the bird, the humans came out and that spoilsport, Peter, took the bird away exclaiming that Pandy certainly had not caught it; he must have just picked it up from somewhere perhaps because it was injured or somebody else had already killed it. A bit of a slur on Pandy's capabilities, I suppose, though very likely true. But in the event it was a lovely thought of Pandy to get hold of the bird - however he managed to do it - and I felt very touched by it.

10.30am Everyone was now sitting on the sunny patio and Sheila and Peter presented me with their present. Well, blow me, it was a lovely heated pad for my bed! They know how much I like the heated bed pads at the holiday camp - sometimes when it's been time to go home they've had to drag me off the pad! Although at this time of the year it wouldn't be used, in the winter months it would be lovely and I knew I would spend many happy, sleepy hours on it. Lois then produced a big pack of mixed tins of the very best make of cat food from some superior store in Knightsbridge in London (so it said on the labels). She gave both Pandy and I a taster and it was certainly whisker-licking delicious I can tell you! We both begged for more but to no avail I'm afraid.

Happy birthday to me, happy birthday to me!

40

11.45am I had gone indoors and was sitting on my favourite chair in Sheila's study when suddenly there was the cacophonous sound of the front doorbell - there must be more chimes than Big Ben in that bell! All the humans were milling around in the downstairs hall, greeting their visitors. The man was flailing his arms about and talking in a most odd accent that I'd never heard before, certainly nothing like the Cornish accents I am used to hearing. I did hear Sheila tell Lois that the newcomers were from somewhere called Essex. The woman was also speaking in the same strange tones. Usually I keep my distance when newcomers arrive, but as this was a special day I decided to go down and investigate. My goodness, the woman was very tall - seemed like a giant to a cat-sized person like me - and she had extremely large feet which at one point nearly crushed me. I decided, though, that they seemed nice, friendly people so as an honour I allowed them to pat me.

12.15pm By this time everyone had moved out into the garden again and the humans were sitting on the patio chairs drinking evil-smelling coloured liquids from a variety of bottles and cans and eating sandwiches and a local favourite, Cornish pasties. Pandy and I were sitting in the sun near to Lois, who was sneaking little bits of pasty to us from time to time. She's good like that. The visitors were all talking rapidly and the words 'ham' and 'eels' caught my attention. Now I am very partial to a nice bit of ham. However, the man kept on talking about how the ham had played recently and I thought, well you eat ham, you don't play with it, what is he talking about! He also kept referring to west ham. I couldn't imagine what he meant - west ham? Does that mean there is an east ham, a south ham and a north ham? It baffled me. Pandy, who doesn't know nearly as much human vocabulary as I do, hadn't a clue what they were on about! Then they started saying how much they liked to eat their own local delicacy - jellied eels. Well, I certainly know about eels, but there again, jellied? What did they mean? As far as I know humans eat jelly which is sweet and fruity-tasting stuff, coloured green or red or yellow. Once, I tried a bit that someone had spilt but it was not at all to my taste. I can't think how a large wriggling eel would let itself be put into a jelly! We used to get eels in the pond at our previous house. I believe they can cross land for short distances and had probably come from the stream that ran through the field next to our garden. Lucky and I quite often used to catch an eel - though they were such slippery devils that it was rarely that we could hold onto one long enough to be able to eat it. We also had some other rather strange land creatures similar to eels in that garden called slow worms. They were great fun to play with because they were easy to catch and you could bite off the end bit and then the two bits would wriggle separately! They used to keep we cats amused for hours. I would often smuggle one (in pieces) indoors to give Sheila a fright. It was worth the telling-off I got seeing her jump up and screech when she trod on one of the wriggly pieces I'd carefully placed on the floor!

3.00pm Peace again - the humans had all gone out. Pandy and I remained sleeping in the garden. I was feeling so content that I almost enjoyed him being alongside me!

6.30pm The house was full of humans again - they seemed to be everywhere. And so noisy all together with music playing and the clinking of glasses again. It seemed to me that the more they drank of the sickly-smelling stuff in those glasses, the more they all seemed to be laughing. Really it was enough to give you a headache. Anyway, Sheila called me into the kitchen and there was the Essex lady all excited with a jar in her hands. She tipped the contents into my dinner bowl saying that it was my birthday treat from them - jellied eels. I looked in the bowl. At least there was no red or green jelly in it. I sniffed at it suspiciously. It didn't smell that bad, but not that good either. As they were anxiously looking at me for some reaction, I decided to take a bite. Well it was certainly an acquired taste, but not as bad as I'd imagined. I'd eaten bits of raw eel, of course, straight from the pond, but not eel preserved in this special way. I ate about half of it which seemed to make the Essex lady very happy. Well, it was kind of her to bring it specially for me but, to be honest, give me a Cornish crab any day! Still, I expect humans in Essex eat very differently from those in Cornwall.

9.30pm The humans had just about finished their dinner and the table was littered with plates, bowls and glasses. I say again, why on earth do they use so many bowls? One each would be sufficient. Cats do not have to spend hours washing up or clearing tables; that's how sensible we are - one bowl per cat. If Sheila thought the same way, she'd only have had to wash up five bowls and five glasses - a two-minute job - rather than having a full dishwasher after just one meal!

11.55pm Well, at last the humans all departed upstairs to bed down for the night and it was peace for me. Listening to them talking and laughing non-stop for the last few hours was keeping me from sleeping and beginning to make my eardrums rattle! But they had all patted me and wished me a happy birthday and the nice thing was, I knew they meant it. I laid down on my bed thinking what a good day it had been and how lucky I had been with my birthday treats. All in all it has been a very good week and I will remember this special day in particular.

I do hope you have enjoyed reading about my week - I look forward to tomorrow and all the other days ahead. I may even become closer to Pandy - you never know!

ONE YEAR ON

BRINGING YOU UP TO DATE!

Hello people - well this is Truffles again, one year on from when I let you first see my diary! I was most gratified that so many of you bought it and enjoyed it! For those of you who never read it, shame on you! Go out and get it! My fans from the first book may want to skip the intro - but for those who never read it, here is a brief note of my background, and this time I shall be telling you more about my pals from the past!

I am now seventeen years old, which is eighty-something in your human years, but I only admit to old age very slowly creeping on, as my fur is as thick and glossy as ever and I have no aches and pains yet and can still put on a turn of speed when I want to. However, as I have my personal carers to attend to my every whim, most of my time now is spent just lazing around, sleeping and reminiscing over events from the past. In this second part, I am going to recall more amusing things that have happened over the years. The older you get the further back your memory seems to go, so I can remember even more things now than I could last year!

First of all, I must give you the cast list! The most important first - me! The others follow!

My friend Tansy and I were picked from a cats' refuge when we were only six weeks old by our human carers, Sheila and Peter. Both Tansy and I had been abandoned with our other siblings, but I do not want to dwell on our short lives before that. Suffice to say that the good life really began when we were taken back to Peter and Sheila's place in Cornwall where we joined a household of various other cats, a St Bernard dog, a macaw and tropical fish indoors and pond fish outdoors. Something for all tastes really - fur, feather and fin.

I am a tabby with an immaculate, evenly striped coat of co-ordinating tans and browns, while Tansy wore a black-and-white long-furred catsuit. The other cats were Lucky, who was pale ginger and white; Taro, an aristocat, who called himself a Birman and who had a super couture coat of pale cream with a seal trim; and finally Robbie, who was a bright shade of ginger and white. Sadly Robbie only had one eye due to a tumour, but this never seemed to bother him and actually didn't make him look odd - he just looked as if he was winking at you!

The place in Cornwall was terrific for all of we pets: a large garden of about ¾ acre that had lots of vegetation and hiding places - a shrubbery, flower beds and rockeries - bordered on one side by a large natural pond of about 60 metres in length and 10 metres across with an island in the middle, and on two other sides by open fields with horses in one and occasionally young cows in the other. We felt as if we were living in a park, and Robbie, in particular, who had spent most of his earlier life, being adopted, living in a small town flat, was always amazed at the open expanse of grass. He thought he was in paradise. When he first joined the gang he was quite frightened of this large expanse of bright green. Up until then all he could remember was being indoors with an elderly human all the time and the only view he got of the great outdoors was looking through a window at a narrow street.

Readers of my diary will know that Lucky, who was ever my preferred companion over all the others, was a fount of knowledge and spent hours telling me about things that had happened both to himself and to other previous pets in the family. So in this little book I freely admit that most of the anecdotes I mention that had occurred before I arrived on the scene were told to me by Lucky. For example, he said that Sheila and Peter some time earlier had two other cats called Sasha and

Coco. They were half-sisters but couldn't have looked more unalike. Sasha was a very long-furred, pure white glamour puss with one blue eye and one green eye. Coco was a dark brown tortoiseshell colour, also long furred. They originated from Liverpool (as did posh Taro coincidentally) and Lucky used to say that his broad Cornish accent and their Liverpool ones, together with Taro's rather affected hoity-toity tones, made up a really interesting cats' chorus! Sasha and Coco moved to the big house and garden together with Taro and Lucky initially, but sadly both of them had passed on to that big cat basket in the sky just before Tansy and I were taken in.

The St Bernard dog was called Hennessy, and Lucky told me that he came into the humans' household as a six-week-old pup to join their basset hound, Lady, who was getting on a bit in years. Lady, the humans thought, would be a good influence on Hennessy and help to train him. Well, said Lucky, that was a laugh! She was as dim as a Toc H lamp and he wasn't much better! However, she perked up when Hennessy was around and Sheila always said it probably extended her life. Lady sadly didn't make it for the family's move to the country house - pity, because she would have been in seventh heaven wandering around the huge grounds sniffing here, there and everywhere.

The feathered member of the group was Geronimo, the blue and gold macaw. He was a real pain to we cats - always shouting and screeching and saying things that really well-bred felines wouldn't dream of uttering. However, we did remember certain words he shouted at us and stored them up in case we ever needed to use them in a real cats' shouting match!

That foul-mouthed bird!

Now, of course, the human carers and I have moved away from our previous home and are ensconced in a different part of Cornwall - still very pleasant, but with a much smaller garden. My needs are fully met, however, as we have a delightful patio area and that is all I really want nowadays - something warm to snooze on. Some good weather would help - it's been a bit lacking this spring so far, but hopefully we look forward to a good summer dose of those lovely warm rays of sunshine.

My neighbour, Pandy, the wimp with the limp, is still around, of course, but now they have two new additions to their family: two lovely young kittens called Milly and Lily arrived just after Christmas.

Well, that is the cast now introduced, so over this coming week, as I once more record my daily activities for your interest and, I hope, amusement, I shall get the memory into gear and try to recall more funny things from the past to tell you.

Sunday:

8.30am Well things haven't changed for the better over this past year as far as my too early wake-up call is concerned. Peter came noisily into the kitchen, disturbing me as usual, and then proceeded to hustle me out of my comfy bed and show me the open door into the garden. Well, he showed it to me - and I looked at it - but in no way was I going out! It was far too early and also that nasty wet dew all over the grass did not encourage me in the least. So I sat firmly on my backside just inside the door and waited whilst he brushed the carpet around my toilet area and changed yesterday's cat litter. In my diary last year I let slip the fact that I rather enjoyed the pastime of scattering litter around as far as I could so that I could also enjoy watching him bending up and down and brushing it all up again. Unfortunately, Peter read this and it motivated him into buying me a new enclosed litter box. This monstrosity is rather like an igloo and with just the small entrance at the front it is now far more difficult for me to scoop bits of litter out. However, I do my best and I'm pleased to say there is always something outside of it for him to sweep up.

8.45am The bits of litter duly tidied and the fresh granules loaded into the igloo, Peter now morphed into my coiffeuse and, with comb and brushes to the fore, he lifted me onto the table and gave me my weekly fur-do. I quite like this procedure; well, the brushing part - not so sure about the comb, particularly when he is combing out the odd tangle in my tail or trousers. I saw a large heap of old fur gradually mounting on the tabletop. I seem to be moulting a lot this year - perhaps this is a sign of a good, hot summer approaching. Anyway, five minutes or so later, I emerged a new cat with my catsuit shining nicely in the rays of the morning sun that were now pouring through the kitchen window and back door (the latter still open in Peter's vain attempt to get me outside!)

9.00am At last the best bit of the morning procedure, breakfast. Today it was a pâté of salmon and herbs - quite refreshing on an early summer's day and I soon finished it off. Peter had disappeared into the part of the house where his motor machines live, so I was left alone in the kitchen to wash my face and whiskers and do my general ablutions. Sheila had still not appeared - she loves her bed as much as I love mine!

9.10am I decided I would, in fact, put my nose out of the back door since Peter was not there to harass me or to see that I had succumbed to his wish of getting me outside in the first place. A cat should never, but never, make the human carers think he/she is under their power. Cats do things THEY wish to do, not what other people want them to do. If the cat's wishes and the human's coincide, well all that does is to make the humans think they DO have the power, but of course we all know that they do not! Over hapless dogs maybe, but certainly not we cats!

9.15am I sat on the back-door mat and enjoyed the sun for a while. Then all of a sudden I noticed Pandy, my admirer from next door, limping towards me. As readers of my previous book will know, he worships the ground I walk on and if I walked on water he would probably drown trying to follow me there too! Such a pity he is not a better figure of a cat - he has this disability with his walking, probably caused by a car accident when he was young or he may even have been like it since birth. Nobody seems to know. I do not mean to be unkind - he is actually quite good looking and wears his immaculate black-and-white catsuit rather well and with a certain style. People often compare him to a certain cartoon cat who advertises cat food. Despite the fact that he is something of a loner and quite often spends the nights outdoors curled up on the earth under bushes or cuddled into a nice comfy compost heap, his white bits always look squeaky clean and his claws are neat and short. I always notice these things, being very fussy about cleanliness myself. Unlike dogs, generally cats keep themselves extremely clean of their own volition, and for cats living in human environments as pets, this also avoids the necessity of their being given the horrid wet baths that dogs have to endure.

9.30am Pandy lay down on the patio a few paving stones away from me with his head on his paws, surveying me. Perversely, even though I am not really attracted to him myself, I felt glad that my coat was newly groomed and that I looked at my best in the sunlight. My variegated brown and golden stripes shone in rather a delightful manner and he was obviously transfixed and probably envious. Even though I am many years older than him, we ladies of a certain age have a particular pride in being able to attract a toy boy. However, it has only really been Lucky, a real swashbuckling hero of my cat world, who has ever attracted me. Lucky was part of our group at the previous house, and in this year's diary most of the stories I intend to tell you were told to me by him when we were snuggled up together during the winter evenings. Though we were close, we were not that close since we were both missing certain parts, which was the one power that Sheila and Peter did have over us! They did not wish for any more cats than their chosen few, and I suppose I can understand this - after all, there will never be another Truffles!

11.00am Well, I was still lying on the patio and I must have been in quite a deep sleep because I never heard Sheila emerge out of the kitchen and it was only when she nearly stepped on me whilst bringing out the washing to hang out that I saw her. Talking of washing - this is yet another human example of wasting time and energy. Why on earth do they need so many different outer coverings? No wonder they get fed up with all the washing and ironing of these unnecessary items - Sheila is always moaning on about how she loathes ironing. Cats never have to do ironing! With just one catsuit, all you need is to give yourself an all over wash each day and your fur comes up sparkling and there is just no need for all this excess. Will humans never understand? They just use up so much energy on these thankless tasks - cats are infinitely more sensible regarding these things.

1.30pm Lunchtime and I wandered back in and found a snack waiting for me in my bowl. Sheila and Peter had gone out to meet some other humans for their own lunch. Sheila always tries to get out of cooking their Sunday roast by suggesting that the one provided in that local place, where humans like to drink those awful sickly drinks, is much better than the one she can prepare.

1.40pm Lunch finished, I strolled into the dining room and settled down on my rug in front of the patio doors, which is my favourite place to sleep, daydream and remember. Pandy positioned himself outside and we both slept.

4.30pm I awoke, had a nice stretch and prepared to recall some moments from the past. You remember that I told you that Sheila and Peter have had several cats. Well, their first pets were two half-sisters called Sasha and Coco. I heard all about them from Lucky, but they had departed for the big runway and taken off to the giant cat basket in the sky before I came on the scene. Lucky told me that Sheila had worked in an office and they had a head office in Liverpool (some other place that I don't believe is in Cornwall) and she got friendly with another human who worked there and kept lots of cats. Sasha arrived first and Coco the following season. Sasha was snowy-white with a very large and fluffy tail (useful in the summer for keeping the midges away!), but Coco was a tortoiseshell colour with - unlike my nice, even, symmetrical stripes - odd patches of colours ranging from pale gold to dark brown. Sounds rather a mishmash to me, but Lucky said she looked quite unusual and everyone seemed to remark on her. Unlike Sasha, who was very elegant and behaved in a ladylike manner, Coco was rather a tomboy. She often got into trouble and Lucky remembered that one day, whilst the humans were out, Coco was investigating a wash boiler, which rather resembled a huge cooking saucepan with a lid. In this receptacle some of Peter's jeans were soaking prior to the - as I mentioned earlier - thankless human task of being washed. At this time Peter was a commercial fisherman (more of that later) and these jeans used to reek of fish when he got home - a wonderful aroma for cats, but obviously not to Sheila; hence the soaking they used to get! Anyway, Coco somehow trod on the lid of this contraption, which immediately turned over and tipped her right into the body of the boiler.

A soggy looking Coco!

Fortunately the soapy water was cold. Coco was suspended somehow by her front paws, clinging for dear life onto the rim of the boiler. In no way could she manage to scramble out. Her long fur was plastered to her and this made her look like a stick insect with just her cheek fur and fur around her face and head remaining dry and fluffy! How long she was trapped like this they were never sure, but Sheila found her when she returned from work - YES she did work in those days! Anyway, consternation when Coco was discovered and she was hauled out and dried off and given some TLC. Well, she learnt her lesson - be careful where you tread, a rule that as a cat she should automatically have known. Still, we can't all be perfect I know - I am pretty well near it myself but even I have made mistakes at times!

5.00pm Sheila and Peter arrived home so I went to greet them, relieved that this time they had not brought any of their friends home. I was still sleepy and in a reminiscing mood, so some strangers in the house would have spoiled the quiet atmosphere I needed to reflect and remember times gone by. They made some of that hot brown stuff humans like to drink and sat outside to consume it, surrounded by the Sunday newspapers. I returned to the mat and tuned in the memory again ...

5.45pm I was thinking about Sasha and Coco and the dog they had to contend with at that time, which was a basset hound called Lady. They must have had an easier time with her, though, than I did coping with a St Bernard and his clumsiness, coupled with his constant drooling over my catsuit!

Yuk!

Rainhat needed here!

Lady was the owner of a pair of the longest ears that Lucky (who, of course, was the one who told me about all this) had ever seen. When she was taken for a walk around the village, sniffing and snuffling all the time (bassets are habitual vacuum cleaners!), she would sometimes step on her ears and trip up, much to the mirth of passers-by. When she was eating she had to have a special bowl with sloping sides so that her ears didn't drag into her dinner, but even this didn't work all the time and Sheila sometimes had to clip her ears together with a clothes peg above her head to keep them out of the way! One day, Lucky said, Sheila was standing at the cooker and felt something pushing against her and, on looking down, she saw that Lady's pegged-back ears had slipped down in front of her forehead, covering her eyes, so Lady, temporarily blindfolded by her ears, had stumbled into Sheila. Honestly, can you believe that a dog could be so stupid! Well, on reflection, yes I suppose you can! There is just no comparison between a cat and a dog - even the brightest dogs cannot measure up to a cat!

7.30pm Well, time for my dinner so into the kitchen I went. Beef chunks tonight - not bad, though I've tasted better.

8.00 - 11.00pm Sat on Sheila's knees whilst they stared at the large oblong-shaped silver box in the corner of the lounge. I've said it before - I just do not understand how they are so transfixed by this box. They sit for hours every evening watching it - well, she does. Peter doesn't seem to be able to keep his eyes open for more than twenty minutes or so before he falls asleep, making those revolting - and sometimes quite frightening to a small cat person like me - roaring and whistling noises. How Sheila stands it I don't know, but as she is only half watching the box and also doing various word and number puzzles (using my back as a resting place for her newspaper), perhaps she manages to close her ears to the rumblings echoing over from Peter's direction.

11.15pm Bedtime, and I sank thankfully into my comfy bed and prepared to dream the rest of the night away. Tomorrow would be another day and I would try to recall more memories from the past.

Monday:

6.30am Well, I could tell it was a weekday (workday for Peter) again, as my wake-up call was at this, such an unearthly and most unacceptable, hour. Today, though, he seemed not quite so enthusiastic as usual about even his own early start. Something about hating Monday mornings I think he was muttering to himself. He really quite briefly attended to my litter box and then dumped my breakfast dish and refilled water bowl in front of me in quite a brusque manner I thought. Not what I am usually accustomed to - I demand respect at all times from my human carers. Normally I get their deference, but occasionally they do get the odd moody on, and today, I realised, was one of these times with Peter. So, to be on the safe side, I tried to look enthusiastic when he showed me the back door and, in that very slow-motion action that we cats are so good at doing, I did poke my nose outside and finally went out onto the patio. In fact it wasn't a bad day and the sun was already trying to force its rays through the leaves on the surrounding trees - it looked as though later on we would have a nice, warm day. I sat down, surveying things in general, whilst Peter had his breakfast.

9.30am Peter had been long gone when Sheila eventually swanned downstairs and into the kitchen where I was now sitting in a sunny patch, basking in the warmth of the sun coming through the windows. After our normal affectionate greeting, she gave me a second helping of breakfast and we sat companionably together for a while. Then, after a sigh, she got up, went to the hall cupboard and fetched out a cumbersome machine on wheels with a handle and brushes underneath it, which I absolutely loathe. Dear readers, I have to put paw on heart and admit to you all that I am totally scared of these awful machines - I always have been, ever since I was a kitten. I don't know why - the other cats didn't seem to mind it so very much, but for some reason it has been a lifelong fear of mine. Now I am not one to admit to anything that might detract from my public image of a cool, calm persona of the cat world, but I'm afraid I do hold up my paws to this one phobia.

10.15am Sheila knows of my fear of the procedure she was now going to carry out, so she picked me up and put me upstairs onto my favourite seat in her study where I always feel safe and secure. She then went down and switched on the infernal machine, which made a most dreadful racket - whirring and humming like a huge swarm of angry, outsized wasps. Whilst I was safely away from the machine I did creep out of the study and peeped down through the banisters to see exactly what she was doing with it. She was in the hall below, striding up and down. I've always wondered about why she does this and I still cannot for the life of me think what she sees in it! I thought at one time that perhaps it gives her pleasure - for why else would she do it? - but I don't think it does, because when she comes to put the horrible thing away she nearly always says, "Well thank God that's done for the week!" She walks up and down all the rooms pushing this thing before her - and that's it! When she leaves a room, nothing looks different to me. What a pointless thing to do. I will never understand humans and their whims.

Before she usually does this, she has previously gone around the same rooms brandishing a bright yellow piece of cloth and flapping it over and around most of the things in the room. Sometimes, if I am watching closely and the sunlight is shining into the room, I see little clouds of small grey particles rise up, but then, as she passes by, well, they all fall back into the same place again! Another ridiculous and pointless pastime. And she repeats this each week. Why? If it's done one week, surely there's no need to keep on and on doing it. It all beats me. Cats would in no way expend their energy in doing such futile and thankless tasks. What a waste of valuable sleeping or eating time.

11.00am Sheila was now lounging in a garden chair drinking out of a tall mug with steam coming from froth at the top of it, a chocolate biscuit bar named after we cats beside her, and a pile of celebrity magazines, which I know she likes to paw (do you get the pun?) through. I sat nearby, relishing the sun and wondering why Pandy from next door hadn't appeared so far today. Still, I didn't want to tire my mind thinking of him; I was still in reminiscing mode. I was trying to remember more tales of the past that Lucky had told me.

12.30pm We were still in the same places. Sun getting even hotter - it really was a super day and, as Cornwall is often quite a damp place, we were making the most of it. I felt quite hot in my rather heavily furred catsuit, but unfortunately there are no zips in it so I couldn't take it off. Sheila, on the other hand, was sitting in quite a skimpy top and shorts. I wish she wouldn't wear the latter - they don't do her any favours at her age. Still, I do know that she wouldn't wear them in public nowadays, which is probably a relief to the rest of the human race, but with just me around, she doesn't care.

2.00pm Lunch over and the heat still rather hot, I had retired indoors and made myself comfy in the dining room again, and now I am going to tell you a bit more about Sasha the white cat and also Geronimo the blue and gold macaw. Sasha was a real glamour puss, though some people thought the fact that she had one green and one blue eye rather strange. However, I believe that this is quite common in white cats and also they tend to go a bit deaf in old age. Lucky never mentioned if Sasha became hard of hearing or not. That could be used to a cat's advantage I would have thought - no need ever to come in when you are called on the excuse that you couldn't hear! Anyway, I digress. Sasha was the queen of scallops! When Peter used to be a commercial fisherman, he would bring home all sorts of fishy things. Lucky could even recall a lobster crawling through the hallway one day with the three cats trailing behind it - not that any of them would have actually dared to tackle a brute like that with such heavy and sharp claws. Funnily enough, it is a human conception that all cats love fish; some do, of course, but most would prefer meat. Sasha was the exception to the other cats in the house at that time, i.e. Coco and Lucky. She was the only one that liked fish. Peter used to bring home bags of scallops and would stand at the kitchen sink removing the shells and cleaning them, while Sasha would sit on the draining board beside him and put her paw into the sink, right into the water, which reached up to her armpit, and hook up scallop after scallop. She could eat up to six or seven at a sitting! Friends of Peter and Sheila, who paid quite a lot to eat scallops in those eating places where humans congregate, were always horrified that a cat could also eat posh nosh but for free!

5.00pm Well, I must have nodded off - all this memory work is tiring! I glanced outside and saw a large magpie on the lawn. That reminded me of when Coco brought one in through the cat flap one day. She was only a few months old at the time and the magpie was as large as she was, if not larger. No way could she have killed the magpie herself, so the humans assumed she had found it recently dead somewhere and just dragged it in. Well, she tried to drag it through, but it got jammed in the opening alongside her. The noise of the flap banging to and fro brought Sheila running and, in due course, Coco and the magpie were freed - Coco to run back to the garden to see if there were any more around, the magpie to the dustbin. Talking of birds made me think of Geronimo, the horrendous macaw! After supper I would recall things about him.

8.00pm Supper duly eaten and in my comfy spot on Sheila's knee, it was time for me to remember things about Geronimo. Peter, Lucky told me, had always wanted a parrot. He and Sheila had had cockatiels, lovebirds and a cockatoo before (not all at the same time!), but this time Peter wanted a large parrot - well, you couldn't get much larger than Geronimo! Sheila rather fancied a toucan, but in the end, as toucans don't imitate humans' speech, they decided on a blue and gold macaw. In the event, we cats would have much preferred a dumb toucan rather than the loud-mouthed macaw, but we didn't have much choice in the matter! The first thing Geronimo (that was the name given to him in the pet shop) did was to learn the cats' names. He then constantly called in his raucous tones, "Saaaashaaa!" and "Cocooooh" and "Luckeeee", and they were forever running in thinking they had been summoned by the humans! Eventually they learned not to be fooled by the noisy bird! He lived in an enormous cage most of the time, but from time to time the humans took him out with them. When he was safely in the cage, Coco, Sasha and Lucky would venture quite near to see this giant bird (as big as a cat) up close and personal, but if they put their paws up to the bars of the cage Geronimo would give them a sharp nip. Sasha was enormously daring and would spring on top of the cage and let her paw dangle down temptingly just above Geronimo's head. This was her idea of playing the game of chicken - or, in this case, macaw! She was usually quick enough to retract the paw as his evil beak lunged in her direction, but Lucky said that one day he must have caught her because she never played that game of chance again. As I said, Geronimo could imitate human speech and he said all sorts of things apart from calling the cats. Sometimes these things came out at very odd moments and caused hoots of laughter from the humans. At that time Peter and Sheila did not have a motor machine and they used to catch the bus to the gathering place where humans drink those disgusting cans and glasses of coloured liquids, which tend, after due course of time, either to make them giggly and stupid or cross and stroppy. I can never think why humans do this. Pure, fresh water or milk are the best things anyone can drink and they have no ill effects, only good ones. Each to his own I suppose, but there again is a reason why in cat years we live so much longer than humans - we look after our diets and don't consume stuff that harms us or makes us do silly things. Anyway, as I said, they would catch the bus with Geronimo stowed away in a wicker laundry basket, which was large enough to enclose him plus his long tail. One day Sheila was on the bus with the basket, Peter beside her, and the other passengers had no idea there was a macaw inside. Suddenly the familiar raucous tones came up with "What are you doing? Stop it, you old bugger!" The passengers all stared at Peter, thinking he must have been chancing his luck! Peter and Sheila kept straight faces, but the story used to come up quite often when they had friends over. Customers in the communal drinking spots they visited in those days used to love seeing Geronimo and a great fuss was always made of him. People liked to have him sitting on their shoulders and he had a penchant for stealing people's earrings out of their ears, but Lucky used to say that Sheila said he'd never managed to get away with any decent diamonds! Geronimo lived to a ripe old age and was inhabiting part of the conservatory in the next house they lived in - with the large garden - when Tansy and I arrived as kittens to join the family. We were rather in awe of him at first, but we soon became as fed up with him as the rest of the cats did. His continual screeching wore us down (particularly when the signature tune of *Coronation Street* came on), and even when he was asleep he wheezed and snored rather like Peter does now. All in all, we weren't very fond of Geronimo and when eventually, after twenty-five years of living with the humans, he went to a kind of parrot rest home to join many other macaws, we were all delighted and would have thrown our hats into the air if we'd had any! We heard that eventually he died from some sort of respiratory problem in his old age not so very long ago. Certainly his shouting and swearing hadn't affected his longevity!

11.00pm Yawn, yawn - bedtime beckoned. I slipped off Sheila's knee and called into the cat litter igloo en route to my comfy bed. The end of another pleasant day.

Tuesday:

6.40am Here we go again - Peter came into the kitchen awakening me from quite a deep sleep. I must have been dreaming about something good, but for the life of me I couldn't remember what. So I wasn't too cross with him for disturbing me and I was pleased to see that he seemed to be in a better humour today. I even thought I heard him whistle as he went about the daily litter change and clean-up. The sun wasn't shining, so I had no intention of going into the garden and thought I would wait until he had refreshed the litter before I went on it and performed. This, of course, meant that he had to redo the cleaning job again. I like to keep my eye on him to see that he doesn't shirk this task and gratifyingly he redid it without any complaint. This was now making me a little suspicious - why was he in such a good mood? My breakfast was placed before me and I tucked in, keeping one eye on him. There seemed to be a pile of envelopes on the breakfast bar and whilst he ate his breakfast he was opening them and I realised that it was his birthday. Well, as you who read my diary last year will have known, my birthday came up during the week I was writing. I had a very good time that day, so I hoped Peter would enjoy his day too. He disappeared off to wake up his motor machine and I went through the cat flap into the garden. Pandy was already out there waiting for me. I gave him a quick glance that said both "hello" and "keep your distance", which he understood implicitly. I do have him well trained. So we sat on the patio, savouring the early morning air which, though the sun had not penetrated the clouds yet, was quite nice and refreshing.

9.00am Sheila appeared in the kitchen and came out and gave both me and Pandy a few cat crunchy titbits. I like these catty sweeties and Pandy does too. It made us feel quite companionable sitting there together. The sun started to win its battle over the clouds and it really was quite pleasant just sitting and daydreaming the time away. Sheila had disappeared and it sounded like she was using that awful, frightening machine again somewhere in the depths of the house.

11.00am Well, our idyllic time in the garden was rudely interrupted by the arrival of Jason the gardener and his grass-cutting machine, which is even noisier than Sheila's evil machine. Pandy dashed off as fast as he could limp and I quickly went indoors and to my vantage point in the dining room behind the patio doors, where I could feel safe and still make sure that Jason and his sidekick were doing their jobs properly and not missing any blades of grass. Soon the garden looked spick and span again and Sheila was taking the opportunity to have yet another cup of that hot, frothy drink she likes so much, and she had also brought out some more for the gardening lads. They all sat down on the bench and chatted and so I joined them to see what they were talking about. Ah - now I knew why Sheila was looking forward to the rest of the day. Her oldest friend, Lois, was due to arrive and they would all be having a special meal in the evening to celebrate Peter's birthday. Lois comes down to visit each year and we all enjoy her stay here. She generally brings me something nice from a posh store in a place called London, which is somewhere fairly near to where she lives - must be a long way from Cornwall, as it takes her about five hours to drive here in her little motor machine. The machine must look forward to coming here too because Peter always gives it a clean. Lois never seems to do this herself. Peter is for ever cleaning his two motor machines - if Sheila wants to know where he is, she always looks in the motor machines' house first.

1.30pm Lois just arrived. She looked as well as ever and told me I did too. I thought, cut the cackle Lois - where's my pressie? And, of course, she gave it to me. It was some tins of caviar and tuna cat food for upper-class cats. Well, of course, that's me! I ate half a tin straight off - simply divine! So now off to my mat in the dining room to while away the time whilst the humans sat outside and caught up on all their news. I shall have forty winks and then try and recall some things about Hennessy, that old, slobbery St Bernard dog.

4.00pm Well the forty winks stretched out into about four thousand winks in the end, but hey, so what! I have all the time in the world to daydream and remember. You, my friends, on the other hand, may not and want to get on, so here is what Lucky told me about Hennessy when he joined the family. As I said in my introduction, he was a really young pup when Sheila and Peter first saw him and fell under his charms; so small, in fact, that they initially told Sheila's father - who was for ever telling them not to have so many pets - that he was only a Jack Russell! Since he grew at a rate of approximately 10lbs per fortnight, they couldn't keep up that pretence for very long! When he was fully grown he weighed over 200lbs - a giant as far as we cats were concerned, but a gentle giant! Sheila had intended to bring Hennessy home in time for her holiday from work in order to look after him full-time, but his breeder wanted her to take him a week earlier. So she took him to her office for that first week, carrying him in a shopping bag! When he was grown up, he could have carried her around in HIS shopping bag! He was from very good stock, so Lucky said, despite not being very astute, and his great-great-grandfather was a Crufts' champion called Bossy Boots. One of his brothers was sold to humans who lived in that alien country across the great pond, and was despatched to them in his own first-class seat on one of those weird machines with wings that hurtle across the sky from time to time scaring me. Yes, I know, I repeat I am an absolute wimp when it comes to facing humans' horrible mechanical and noisy machines. Hennessy's other brother went to be sold in that enormous and expensive store in London that Lois frequents so often. Hennessy had a very soft temperament and he loved us all - humans and cats alike. I'm not sure whether he liked Geronimo though! Did anybody? Lucky, when he was first brought home, went as if by instinct immediately to Hennessy and snuggled up to him, seeing him right away as a huge cuddly, friendly ally. Indeed he was - to all of us - and quite often we used to sleep curled up beside or on top of him at night rather than in our own baskets. He did tend to dribble a lot over our catsuits and to keep cleaning them repeatedly was a pain at times. He was very clumsy and trod on our tails or paws, which also annoyed us, but he was always a soft touch and meant well, so we couldn't say too many bad things about him. I mean, we cats could run rings round him, so anything we wanted him to do, he did. Mind you, any cat can run rings round any dog - it's a fact of life!

Nothing like a comfy St Bernard to snooze on ...

7.00pm I had just finished my dinner, which was pretty unremarkable, as Sheila seemed more concerned about making sure that Lois was fed better than I was! If this happens again I shall take her to task. I expect gourmet food on a regular basis and the humans know this well - it is clearly set out in my directives. On this occasion, though, I will let it lie, as I know that Lois will be giving me bits and pieces from her dinner plate. When she is here, I sit right by her feet so she can't miss me and give her the penetrating "please feed me" stare that always works. She has no pets of her own, so I am something of a novelty to her and she, quite rightly, thinks I am the cat's whiskers, as they say!

8.oopm The dining room table was covered with multitudinous plates, dishes and drinking vessels (what a wasteful extravagance - one bowl each for food and one bowl for drink is all they really need) and the humans were tucking in to something that looked and smelt like duck to me, though it seemed to be disguised with an orangey, sickly smelling sauce on top of it. I know that Peter has always been very fond of duck, so I guessed this was his birthday treat! Lois duly passed me down several bits of the duck from which, in her thoughtful way, she had scraped off the obnoxious sauce, and they were quite lip-smackingly delicious! Thoughts of my own uninteresting dinner faded away after eating these super morsels!

9.oopm Sheila, Peter and Lois lounged in their chairs, talking non-stop and only pausing every so often to gulp some strange fizzy liquid out of the huge glasses they were holding, and I was beginning to doze but, before I did so, I recalled a story about Hennessy that became a frequently told story around their dinner table for many months after the event. Sheila was out for a walk with Hennessy one day and they were ambling along a narrow country lane hedged tightly in on both sides with thick bramble bushes loaded with blackberries - a favourite spot with the humans in the autumn when they gathered baskets of these odd things that apparently they loved to eat. Certainly they would never appeal to cats or dogs - didn't smell meaty enough for us. Anyway, in the distance, coming towards them, was a female human in a pale blue coat with a small terrier-type dog. They were accompanied by a male human. The dog was trotting on ahead off the lead and the gap between it and Hennessy was closing by the minute. Sheila always held Hennessy on a tight lead - well, his lead was more of a heavy chain that would have probably hauled up a boat off a beach it was so large! Sheila needed it to hold Hennessy back if he wanted to rush off anywhere! Normally he was slow and placid, but other dogs used to think of him as the humans' cartoon hero, "The Incredible Hulk", because he was so very large, and the majority he met during his walks tended to lunge at him to show they were not afraid of his size! They would often be aggressive to try to show they were unafraid, which I bet they were if one only knew the truth! Hennessy didn't care. He loved any dog - large or small - and always would have liked to have had a run round or game with them, but this never happened because of his size. Shame really, because he was never able to enjoy a good romp with any other dog. Lucky said he used to play with him when he was younger and they had some good games of 'chase', but playing with a cat from your family at home is not the same as playing with doggy pals outdoors! Anyway, I digress again, and meanwhile, the humans plus the terrier were fast approaching. Although the people could quite clearly see that Sheila was holding Hennessy firmly on a short lead and keeping him tight to her side, they made no attempt to call their own dog to them or put him on a lead. If they had done this, everyone would have passed one another without incident and they could have let him off again! So, needless to say, the terrier leapt at Hennessy, and he, in turn, lunged forward towards it. Sheila could not hold on to the lead so she dropped it, and Hennessy - in his usual clumsy way - knocked the terrier head over paws, then knocked the female human in the blue coat right into the hedge and followed this up by immediately also knocking the male human into the opposite hedge! What a commotion! Sheila rushed after

Hennessy and quickly grabbed him, checked that the others were all back on their feet again and shouted apologies and they all continued their separate ways, the other two humans literally not saying a word. They must have realised that they should have called their little dog back rather than let it provoke Hennessy, which surely they must have guessed would cause trouble! No sense, some humans! Anyway, the twist in the tail of this little episode was that about three months later Sheila and Peter were at a gathering of humans in their next-door neighbours' house and the couple in the lane were also there! Sheila recognised them immediately and quickly melted away to another part of the room, hoping they would not recognise her!

11.00pm Well, the droning of the humans' voices plus some pleasant background music, coupled with a tummy full of bits of duck, has made me sleep for the past hour or so - I have to keep up my sleep pattern whatever the circumstances. A cat tries to sleep at least 22 hours out of 24 and I generally succeed. Another reason why I am so well preserved for my age - I have never overexerted myself. My batteries are always being freshly recharged during my sleep periods!

11.45pm A rather late night for me but at last the others had all gone upstairs to their own beds. The stuff in the glasses seemed to have made them very giggly. Goodness knows why. As I said earlier, drinking milk or water doesn't make cats giggly! I slid into my bed and looked forward to some more sweet dreams and the prospect of another pleasant day tomorrow.

Wednesday:

6.40am Peter came rather quietly into the kitchen this morning. He seemed very subdued - strange, I would have thought he would have been buoyed up following his birthday celebrations last night! He seemed to be holding his head and for once didn't try to make me go outside. He also made some groaning noises when he was bending down to see to the dreaded igloo and appeared quite pleased when he realised I had had no need to use it during the night. His breakfast today, I noticed, consisted of a glass of water (much more sensible than that sickly smelling fizzy stuff he was drinking last evening) with a white pill. I wondered if he was giving himself a worming pill? Seems ages since I was last given one by my lovely vet, Mr Kingdon, but I suppose it can only have been about six months ago.

8.00am Peter had eventually disappeared off to work - I'm never really sure exactly what his 'work' is. He doesn't particularly seem to enjoy it. Certainly it's something that we cats wouldn't consider doing. Why work when you keep servants? Sheila and Lois still hadn't appeared downstairs, so I returned to my bed for a while, which of course is no hardship to me! In that pleasant state of being half asleep and half awake, I recalled something else Lucky told me that had happened with Hennessy when he really had got into big trouble with the humans! Being so large, he had a bed that Peter had had specially made for him, as no basket would have been big enough. Lady the basset hound, on the other hand, had had for years a round wicker basket with which she was very happy. (It doesn't take much to make a simple soul like a basset hound happy). Anyway, when Hennessy was a little puppy he made Lady's basket the object of his attentions when he was teething! He chewed large chunks out of the wicker surround until there was literally nothing of it but a base and a few bits of upright stalks. Sheila saw advertised in one of her magazines a "guaranteed completely indestructible" dog beanbag bed, so she thought this would be just the thing for

Lady - a nice, cosy, squashy bed. She duly sent away for it and, one Saturday morning, there was great excitement for Lady when it arrived. It was placed on the floor alongside Hennessy's enormous bed in the cellar room where they both spent their nights, and Lady began the process of examining it and discovering all its comfortable charms. Lucky said that she had told him how excited she was at getting a new bed at last, since Hennessy had ruined her basket. The humans went out for a couple of hours to their local gathering place in the village, thinking what a delightful picture they had left behind them - two happy dogs dozing in their own respective beds. When they returned, however, something of a shock awaited them! The entire room was covered in piles and piles of tiny white beads - so light that every slight draught from the window or the opening of the door sent them flying up and out into every nook and cranny. The "indestructible" bed had several large holes chewed in the cover from which the beads had spewed out! Hennessy was sitting on his bed trying to look invisible, and Lady was mournfully lying by the doorway, wiping her eyes with her ears as she came to terms with the loss of her bed again, without even having had the pleasure of one night's sleep on it!

Lady's perforated bed!

Sheila was furious with Hennessy, needless to say, and the hapless Peter got the task of collecting up all the floating beads, which took him some considerable time, and the air above these beads turned a rather dark shade of blue for some reason that Lucky couldn't quite fathom out! So Lady never did get her super-comfy bed. She managed with another old basket that Sheila had refurbished, as she was not going to waste any more money on something new that Hennessy would ruin. Still, Lady was, as I said, a simple and placid animal, and she never made any great fuss about it. I would have been livid - I take a pride in my possessions. I have two beds, one for the day and one for the night, and I make sure they are regularly cleaned and the covers kept well brushed. Cats will in no way compromise like dogs will. Only the best for us will do!

10.00am I was awakened from my dozing and memories by the sound of the female humans tentatively feeling their way down the stairs. They sat down in the kitchen with hardly a word of greeting for me - very rude I thought - and proceeded to drink some more of the hot stuff they like but this time it was very black in colour and not all frothy as they usually had it. However, they seemed to enjoy it and very soon both of them brightened up a bit and I heard the words "shops" and "shoes" mentioned in the same breath and they disappeared outside and vanished away into the distance in Lois's motor machine.

11.15am I went through the cat flap and settled onto the patio as the sun was now out shining and it was getting nice and warm again. I wondered idly where Pandy could be, but then who should come tippy-toeing by me but the two latest arrivals from next door - Milly and Lily. Sadly, Bob, who I mentioned in my diary last year, is with us no more. A few months after I had finished my diary he was unaccountably knocked over by one of those infernal motor machines and went immediately up to the big cat basket in the sky. His owners were devastated and then, to add to the upset, Ty, who also lived there, decided to move in with some other humans in the area with whom he had formed a great friendship during the daytime whilst the humans in his family were out at their work (tell me, what DO these humans all find so attractive about work?!) So at Christmas two new kittens arrived next door to cheer the humans up. They were the most glamorous kittens I had ever seen - Lily is pale grey-white with very, very long, thick fur and Milly is a few shades darker and more beige in colour. Their tails are to die for - as wide as their bodies! I don't want to sound jealous of their good looks, but I AM! I have always been used to people admiring me and telling me what a nice looking, traditional tabby cat I am, but now, if Milly and Lily are around, all the humans tend to look at them before they realise I am there too. Still, I don't think they are half as talented as I am, so being beautiful is not everything!

Tails to die for!

11.20am I sat and looked at the two glamour pusses and they sat down nearby and shyly smiled at me. In repose, their facial expression makes them look rather cross, as their Persian breed tends to do, but they do have enchanting little smiles when they want to. They are both still 'feeling their feet' as we say, and as yet

75

have not been too far away from their own home. In spite of being only about six months old, they are really quite mature and I just hope that they, in their youthful innocence, do not come into contact with any of the neighbourhood toms who would be delighted to take advantage of them. Nobody ever took advantage of me, needless to say - nobody ever gets the advantage over Truffles! The girls stayed sitting by me for about half an hour and we made desultory conversation about the weather, the state of the lawns, etc. I asked if they had seen Pandy, but they only knew that he had slept out the previous night and had not been back since. He tends to do this in the summer months, finding comfy places where Jason and his friend have stacked up grass cuttings, or snuggling into the centre of clumps of ferns or soft-leaved bushes. No doubt he would turn up soon!

1.30pm Speak of the devil - Pandy ambled up. The girls had long gone. I think Pandy is rather nervous in their company - having never had a girlfriend himself, as far as I know, he doesn't really know how to talk to them. With me, the older, attractive but unobtainable female object of his desire, he is far more at his ease.

1.45pm I was getting a mite hungry - Sheila and Lois were still out, and I had not eaten since breakfast. I examined my bowl again but, however hard I licked at it, nothing was forthcoming. Sheila will be getting a scratch from me if she isn't careful - she has become rather preoccupied with having Lois here and is not paying the attention she should to my wants. This will not do.

2.00pm I returned to the patio and Pandy, my tail beginning to twitch as I felt a touch of anger coming on about this food business. I lay down with my back to Pandy, as I suddenly did not feel in the mood for light chat. I had intended to do a bit more reminiscing, but that would now come later once I had been fed.

2.30pm At last - sounds of the humans returning. Sheila and Lois came into the kitchen and dumped a heap of shopping bags on the floor. I stalked in with my ears not up in their usual welcoming manner but lying somewhat flat, so Sheila could tell something was seriously wrong. We do understand each other very well and, despite the language problem sometimes, I can make her know immediately when I am not satisfied with things. I pointedly walked up to my bowl and she started getting flustered and apologising profusely whilst she decanted some nice-smelling stuff into it from another tin that Lois had brought with her. Okay, I thought, I'll forgive you this time for being late with my lunch, but thousands wouldn't! The lunch consisted of a terrine of simply delicious pheasant and venison, so as I gobbled it up greedily I definitely forgave her! She did go outside and gave Pandy - who by that time was slavering over the smell wafting out to him from my dinner - a little taster of it too, so he was also in ecstasies of delight over it!

2.45pm We all, cats and humans, lay out on the patio companionably side by side - cats dozing, humans chattering. Don't they just go on and on? What on earth do they have to talk about all the time? They never seem to stop and it all sounds so superfluous to me - mostly about hair, those things called shoes that they fix on over their paws, and what the latest human 'celebrities' are getting up to. Boring, boring, boring - still, each to his own I suppose. Cats only make conversation when they have to or there is something important to pass on. As with everything we do, we save our energy and prolong our lives by doing everything in moderation!

4.00pm I will tell you just a couple more incidents that happened with Hennessy and then that will be the end of the dog

77

talk! In any case, cat talk and reminiscences are far more interesting than dog ones, aren't they? The house that the humans were living in when Hennessy joined them was situated in a small village by the sea, and Sheila used to take Lady and him for walks along the top of the nearby cliffs where there was a large expanse of grass for them to run about off the lead. Not that Lady ever ran very much - Sheila would open the gate at the cliff top and would walk right along the path with Hennessy, sit down for a while perhaps, and then come back again to the gate to find Lady still there snuffling the scents that to her seemed so irresistible! Anyway, on this particular occasion Lady was not with them and Sheila was with her father, who was staying with them at the time, and Hennessy. As the trio meandered along this cliff-top path, suddenly a shout from the beach below made them all jump. It was some humans from the village who recognised Sheila's father and were making themselves known. They were the proud owners of two dachshunds who hated the sight of Hennessy and always rushed at him whenever they met in the village. Hennessy, seeing these two little pests, immediately leapt from Sheila's grasp and started dashing straight down the steep side of the grassy dunes, aiming himself right at the two dogs who, in turn, took to their heels and streaked at full speed right across the beach, heading somewhere in the direction of the village! The humans stood momentarily transfixed as their canine pets vanished from view in a puff of sand, followed by a St Bernard hurtling by. Sheila and her father came panting and gasping down the hill and they, plus the other two humans, followed the direction of the three dogs who were by now completely out of sight. By the time they had reached the village, needless to say there were no dogs to be seen. They walked around asking people if they'd noticed two dachshunds running like mad, pursued by a huge St Bernard - not a sight you would think anyone would miss - but their enquiries came to no avail. Sheila fetched Peter out from their house and he walked around searching for Hennessy for quite a while before suddenly he came upon him being led along by one of his human fishermen friends. Apparently this fellow had seen Hennessy ambling along the street and, as everyone knew Hennessy and who he belonged to, he had grabbed his trailing chain - also managing to cut his hand in the process - with the intention of bringing him back home. He had seen no sign of the other two dogs! (Peter and Sheila heard later that apparently they had fetched up at the back of a car park at the end of the village where their owners had one of those houses on wheels parked. The two dogs sat trembling underneath this contraption until their owners found them, but the good thing about this chase was that they learned their lesson and never taunted Hennessy again). But still Hennessy managed to blot his copy book! Whilst Peter was talking to his pal, Hennessy cocked his leg and filled the other human's rubber boot right up! Honestly, would you credit it? Only an uncouth dog would do that kind of rude thing! Can you imagine a cat doing anything like that? No, no, no! We are so clean in our habits. We do not have to be house-trained like dogs - given a special spot to 'go' on, we USE it and even outside in public we make sure we are tucked away out of sight and always, but always, clean up and fill up our toilet holes. I should have thought that Peter's pal must have wished he'd never bothered to catch Hennessy after that little performance!

6.00pm My dinner time, and I enjoyed a nice plate of cod and haddock pieces in jelly. I must say that nowadays there are so many different foods around for cats we are spoiled for choice, but, even so, to us the humans' food always seems to smell that much better - as the saying goes, the grass is always greener over the fence - and I myself particularly like the odd stuff they eat called 'cheese'. I am lucky that they realise this and usually I am given a chunk or two if they are eating some. Tonight they all disappeared out and I was left alone to continue my snoozing and remembering.

9.00pm One more story about Hennessy that I promised you. This time I was around, as it occurred at the big house and garden. It had been a quite normal day and we cats and Hennessy had all been in the garden as usual and the humans were sitting by the pond enjoying the sunset. Suddenly they realised that Hennessy didn't seem to be in sight! They started calling him, but no response. He had never gone missing like that before, so Peter went off one way around the neighbourhood calling, and Sheila the other. However, an hour or so later and they had had no luck. They then decided to go into the communal drinking and meeting place of the local humans to ask there, but on the way they met a friend coming towards them with Hennessy, wearing rather a sheepish look, ambling peacefully beside her! It seemed that Hennessy had somehow got out of the garden and wandered along the road until he came to this place which, because of the nice evening, had its door open in a welcoming manner. Inside, he had gone right up to the bar and had made himself an instant hit with the humans gathered there; hit in more ways than one, perhaps, as - clumsy as ever - he had apparently knocked over several small tables en route and with his ever-wagging, enormous, fluffy tail he'd deftly removed glasses and bottles from the tops of others he'd barged by! But everyone was laughing and nobody seemed to care too much. Various humans had made a great deal of fuss of him and had given him lots of titbits - including cheese (how lucky can you get? Cheese!) and bags of crisps, etc. Because he had no collar on, since at home he didn't always wear it, nobody had known where he had appeared from until Sheila and Peter's friend had arrived. So, luckily again for Hennessy, he was 'rescued' and, from that day on, the humans made certain their gate was shut tight at all times. What a business it must be having to look after a stupid creature like a dog. We cats are far more easy to look after. We don't need constant supervision, or walks, and if we do wander off we are sensible enough to find our own way home again without causing lots of fuss.

11.30pm Loud sounds awoke me from a deep sleep and Peter, Sheila and Lois came back from wherever they had been. I think they had been eating and drinking again - something of a celebratory meal out with the excuse that it was again for Peter's birthday and also because Lois was leaving to go back home again. They came and sat by me and patted me and appeared rather giggly again. I wished they would go upstairs and go to bed and leave me in peace really, but they meant well and thought they were making me happy with their company after leaving me alone all evening. I must say it is nice to feel loved and cared for - you hear of so many ill-treated cats with no comforting human carers - and I know I am blessed with my human family.

12.15am Peace at last - time for bed. Well, I thought it was going to be peace but very soon I was disturbed by the sound of the front doorbell (that awful, loud, clanging sound that makes my fur stand on end!) and the humans' voices somewhat raised. I thought I could also hear some cat cries in the distance, but as nobody came into the kitchen where I was to explain the situation to me, I was kept in the dark - literally! After what seemed an hour but what I suppose was only really about 15 minutes, there was the sound of the front door closing and Peter coming back and going upstairs again. Oh well, I thought, no doubt I will discover what it was all about the following day. I was finding it hard to keep my eyes open, my ears had been straining to no avail, so I slid off into that delightful place I visit every night - slumber land.

Thursday:

6.40am The morning routine had come round again! Peter woke me as usual and tried his utmost to get me to go out into the garden, but this I had no intention of doing - far too early for civilised cats to get up! Then I left him to it - to tidy last night's litter in the igloo, and prepare my breakfast. I know he kicks at this task sometimes, but it is clearly in his job description and there is just no excuse that I will accept for sub-standard work. I always inspect my toilet area, my water bowl and my adjacent eating area, and he knows that if everything is not up to scratch (yes, I know, another awful pun!) I will be certainly giving HIM a scratch to make the point!

7.00am The igloo back in its rightful place, clean litter installed and the carpet around it brushed up, Peter put my breakfast down. I sauntered up to it and sniffed. Well, it didn't smell particularly exciting. I'm not even sure what it was - a kind of mishmash of all sorts flavoured with both fish and meat. I then realised it was one of those cheapy cat foods that Sheila tries to slip to me from time to time, thinking she is saving money. I don't like her being deceitful over things like that and I really must take her to task over it. A cat of my superiority should not have to settle for second best at any time, so this miserable breakfast was just not on. Peter was eating his own breakfast. Needless to say, HIS breakfast was one of the top brands of cereal, not like this OWN BRAND stuff he was trying to inflict on me! I rubbed against his ankles to attract his attention and then walked over to the bowl and tipped it right over! Lovely - bits and pieces all over his newly swept floor. I knew that would bring him to his feet! He was muttering specific words about the behaviour of cats both last night and this morning, including an adjective before the word "cats" that began with the letter F, which I really did not wish to know. However, my ploy worked and after he'd cleared up the mess he did slam down my bowl with some different food in it, which I found to be reasonably acceptable. I did not like his attitude towards me, though, so after I had eaten some of the meal, I pointedly returned to my bed, turned my back and tuned into sleep mode again.

8.15am Peter had stamped out, nearly knocking the kitchen door off its hinges going to his work or wherever he was going to that morning, so I decided to go into the garden and see what was happening out there. I went through the cat flap and was greeted by a rather anxious-looking Pandy, who had obviously been waiting for me on the patio. What did he want? I wondered. Well, whatever it was it would have to wait until I had performed my morning ablutions. I strolled towards the nice flower bed at the back of the garden where I have commandeered several sheltered and pleasant spots as my toilet areas. All these are much better on a warm and sunny day than that horrible igloo structure, but, on the other hand, on a cold and wet day the igloo couldn't be more convenient.

8.30am I arrived back on the patio again, having taken my time on the flower bed as I knew Pandy was so agitated and it would show him, once more, my superiority and that if he wants to speak to me or approach me he has to await my pleasure in these things. When you get to my age it is lovely to have a young admirer but, although underneath I am very flattered and also quite fond of him really, I must never let him see it. Pandy then told me what all the commotion had been about the previous night. Apparently one of the girly kittens, Milly I think he said it was, had got out of one of the upstairs windows of their house, tip-pawed along their roof and then - in a somewhat amazing feat - had leapt across a gap of about two metres to get on top of our roof!

Silly Milly stranded on the roof!

She was clinging on to the gable end for dear life, for she had almost immediately realised that she would not be able to turn round and get herself back again! So she had started screeching for help at the top of her voice! Her humans eventually heard her and came out to see what had happened. There was Milly, voice getting hoarser and hoarser by the minute, in a very perilous position. Why, I say, do so many cats do this silly thing? They climb up tall trees or fences or leap onto roofs and then get themselves stuck! That is something I have never done - I did naturally get into a good few high places when I was younger, but I always had a plan of action and I looked before I leapt and made sure I could always escape or return to where I had started. That is the essential thing a cat should always do - plan, plan and plan. The humans have an expression "as crafty as a cat" and this is essentially very true - of me, certainly! Anyway, the next-door humans rang our doorbell and Peter came out and saw the situation. Fortunately he had a long ladder and soon Milly was rescued and taken back home very shamefaced. Her humans from that day on made sure their upstairs windows were not opened very wide, but I expect Milly learned her lesson from that escapade and, to my knowledge, she has not been in any trouble since!

9.30am Sheila and Lois appeared at the back door. Lois was leaving and had come to say her goodbyes. I was sorry to see her go - but she will be down again next year. She patted me and also Pandy, who likes to get pats from everyone he can. I am more circumspect myself - I only allow my humans and their close friends to touch me. I like to know where everyone has been and who they are before I let them put their huge, clumsy paws on me!

9.35am I followed them indoors and retired to my sunny patch in the dining room behind the patio doors. Time for my morning sleep. Pandy lay down on the patio outside the doors and we drifted off, dreaming our own dreams.

12.30pm My rumbling tummy woke me - Pandy was nowhere to be seen. I strolled into the kitchen and Sheila was already there making herself some nice ham sandwiches. I indicated that I, too, would like some ham and very soon she and I were seated outside on the patio, sun now streaming down on us, agreeably sharing the sandwiches. I must say, it is a cat's life. If one is fortunate enough to have employed the right human carers and they have a comfortable home to share with you, what more can you wish for? It is a pity that so many of we cats (dogs too, of course) are always looking for humans to care for us. When I think right back to the start of my long life, when Tansy and I, as unwanted kittens, were in the animal refuge, it was always packed to capacity. The people who ran it were always desperate for kind humans to take care of the inhabitants, and Tansy and I were lucky that Sheila and Peter took a shine to us and brought us back to share their home. Little did they realise at the time, I suspect, that from then on their whole lives would be taken over by us - but I don't think, in the main, they have ever regretted it.

4.30pm Sheila was lounging on the garden seat, flipping through those magazines about celebrities she enjoys so much - wishes she was one herself I suppose - and I was comfortably ensconced in the centre flower bed with its slate chippings that are so delightfully warm to lie on. Suddenly around the corner came Peter, together with two of their human friends they call Christine and Brian, saying that they were all dying for a cup of that brown stuff they all like to drink. Sheila roused herself and went into the kitchen to get the drinks and the others ranged themselves around on the seats. I looked warily at Christine - she is one of the few people that visit who do not really like cats. Over the years she has mellowed a bit, but the first time she ever came to see Peter and Sheila in the previous house she was visibly quite scared to find herself surrounded by we five cats! Needless to say, we summed up in one minute that she was uncomfortable in our presence and immediately Tansy and I homed in on her. If a cat sees that a human does not like it, it will always make a point of harassing that human by trying to sit right by them, or even on them, to unnerve them. It always works and is a game that all cats like to play. Eventually, in most cases, the human gets worn down, gives in and pats the cat. Everyone is happy - and it's one up to the cat, of course! Today was so hot that I didn't bother removing myself from the flower bed. The others were all chatting and drinking and eating a Cornish speciality - scones with cream and jam. Ah, cream, I thought, and this did inspire me to get up out of the flower bed and move towards Christine in the hope that she would give me a lick of the cream on her scone! In the event, she didn't - the meanie! Sheila took pity on me, though, seeing I was slavering at the sight of all that cream. She put her plate on the ground and in two ticks I was on to it, licking off all the cream she had left on it. Delicious, gob-smackingly delicious, it was too. Nothing to beat a good dollop of Cornish clotted cream, I say! Then Peter quite spoilt the euphoric moment by saying that 'the cat' (I mean, what did he mean 'the cat' - it's Truffles here, you know, not just 'the cat'!) should not be allowed to eat off her plate! Well, that's a sauce! We cats are amongst the cleanest creatures on the planet - always licking ourselves all over from top to tail and keeping scrupulously clean at all times - and here's him saying in a very discriminatory way that we shouldn't eat off their plates! Well, I certainly wouldn't want him, or any other human for that matter, eating off MY plate, but to say that 'the cat' should not eat off their plates - what a cheek! Well, I was totally affronted! You could say that my front was totally put out! I felt really uptight, so I stalked off and went into my bed and prepared to have a sulk, but Sheila followed me in and calmed me down and said I should not take Peter's comments to heart. It was just a principle kind of thing - he did NOT think I was just 'the cat', but he did have strict rules of hygiene and really she should have remembered that and put the cream into my own bowl. Christine had followed Sheila in and was nodding her head to all this - but then, she wouldn't understand would she? Not being a cat person she probably classes us all as 'unclean' animals like dogs are. Well, it would take me a while to stop bristling over all this and so they both tactfully returned to the garden and I curled up and started to count to a hundred but somehow never reached it - sleep overcame me again! I think I have mentioned before that cats try to sleep at least 22 hours out of 24, and I certainly have always adhered to that custom!

7.30pm I awoke and saw that the friends had gone and Peter and Sheila were eating their supper in the kitchen. When Peter saw I was awake he did have the decency to apologise for his little outburst and, as the intervening sleep had calmed me down, I graciously accepted his apology and purred at him to say I also apologised for getting a strop on, and had forgiven him completely. I love him dearly, but I know he has some funny ideas - like this example of thinking that humans care more about hygiene than cats - so at times, to keep the peace, we all have to compromise with each other. My dinner was already in the bowl (mine!) and this time it was one of the posh tins that Lois had given me, so I had no complaints there. It was squid rings, Mediterranean style, so eating this gourmet meal quite put me in the best of humour again. I was ready to love everyone and everybody!

8.00 - 11.15pm Sat on Peter's knee for a change this evening whilst they carried on with their usual evening's entertainment of watching the box in the corner of the lounge. I could have done with some earplugs once he started his snoring and wheezing, but mercifully, despite that, I soon dropped off myself, but not before I remembered one more event, that could also perhaps be classed under the category of 'hygiene disasters'. This concerned Hennessy when they were living in the house by the sea, and Lucky, once more, had related this to me. Hennessy was still quite young and sometimes very boisterous, particularly when other humans visited the house and he was greeting them. On this occasion, there had been some kind of problem in the back yard and some men earlier in the day, dressed in trendy, matching overalls, had been doing strange things with long pipes and brushes, all of which they were feeding down into a large square hole outside the back door. Lucky said the hole appeared to be full of a brown-coloured liquidy substance and odd things like pink bits of paper were floating on top of it. Lucky did not know what these things were, but they didn't smell particularly nice to him so he didn't care to examine them too closely. The workmen were sitting down having a meal break when somebody knocked at the front door. Sheila answered the door and in came some friends who, of course, knew Hennessy and patted him and greeted him most affectionately. Hennessy got all excited and bounded back along the passage to the back door, which led down three or four steps. Down he bounced and fell right into the square hole up to his neck! Well, the smell was horrendous! Hennessy scrambled out, covered in thick brown sludge and festooned with bits and pieces of the pink paper hanging off his tail and caught around his ankles. He then galloped around the back yard before one of the workmen, wearing huge rubber gloves, caught hold of him. All the humans were either screaming, shouting or laughing, or doing all of these things at once! Lucky, Sasha and Coco removed themselves upstairs pretty darn quick and Hennessy was hosed down by the humans with lots of water. The whole of the back yard was quite flooded for a while, but it seemed that Hennessy falling into the pit had somehow cleared it of its revolting contents. The workmen's job was done, Hennessy was dried off, the back yard was washed down and swept, the visitors went, and when Peter arrived home from work an hour later he said to Sheila, "Hello dear, had a good day?" He never understood why she threw a towel at his head!

11.25pm Bedtime. Another day over. Sleep beckons once more.

Friday:

6.30am Thank goodness it's Peter's last 'working' day of the week and I won't get woken at this horrible hour tomorrow - two days' respite with two extra hours in bed! Saturdays and Sundays are definitely the best in the week for me. I looked around and through the cat flap and, yes, another nice, sunny day seemed to be dawning. In fact, to my own - let alone Peter's - surprise, I decided to go right into the garden and attend to my ablutions. He was quite amazed, or perhaps amused, that he didn't have to coerce me into going out so early! I left him to do my housekeeping chores and strolled around the perimeter of the grass. That was still too damp with dew for me to put my paws on. I would wait until the sun had dried it up later. Continuing around the edge, I found a sheltered spot on the flower bed and was soon engrossed in the first performance of the day. I had just finished and was adjusting my catsuit and covering up, when the two young glamour pusses from next door came by. Milly was still a little quiet after her recent excursion onto our roof, but Lily was full of it! She had spotted a rather dashing, black-furred, oriental-looking tomcat peering at her through the back hedge with the biggest pair of golden eyes she had ever seen. She wanted to know if I knew anything about him. Well, I said, yes he certainly has tried to mesmerise me in the past with those huge eyes. But I am past all this lovey-dovey business now, so I had just smiled my Cheshire cat, enigmatic smile and gone on my way. Again, it was nice to know that even at my age I could still attract an eligible male, but, as I've mentioned before, if I had ever decided to get serious, Lucky would have been the only one for me. I indicated to the girls where the oriental charmer lived and they pit-pattered over the damp grass and disappeared in his direction. I returned to the kitchen and my breakfast - food is far more exciting than romance nowadays!

6.50am I wasn't disappointed - breakfast was shrimps in a light, creamy sauce. It soon disappeared - not even a morsel left for Pandy, who generally receives all my leftovers. Perhaps Sheila could fob him off with the remnants of the own-brand revolting stuff I had rejected the other day! I don't suppose he would care - I don't think he is fussy. Any extra food he can con the gullible humans out of is a bonus to him! Somehow he works it so that he gets two breakfasts, two lunches and two dinners per day - his own plus whatever my humans give him. His acting is definitely worth an Oscar. He has perfected the art of looking dejected and unwanted, starving and lonely. Sheila and Peter fall for it every time. Even today I noticed that Peter had placed a bowl outside the back door for Pandy with what bits I had left from my last night's supper.

8.00am I inspected the igloo and surrounding area and it seemed Peter had done his job quite well. He had gone off to see his beloved motor machines. I can't see what he sees in noisy, frightening metal monsters like those, but he spends a lot of time with them in their quarters attached to the front of our house, and is always washing and polishing them. He soon disappeared in one of them and peace reigned. I got back into bed for another quick nap before Sheila came down.

9.30am Down she wandered and on went the noisy little machine in which she makes her hot, frothy drinks. By this time the sun had taken his hat off and was really bright and it was obviously going to be a very hot day - I sighed and wished that on occasions like this I could remove my catsuit. Unfortunately, as I told you earlier, the makers never thought to put any zips in it! Anyway, we went outside and Sheila sat on the seat and I lay under it, grateful for the shade. Pandy very soon joined us and lay down a few patio slabs away, keeping one eye on me, as I was doing on him!

Keeping our distance!

The three of us sat quietly and peaceably idling the morning away. I began to recall past events again and I remembered it was a lovely day like this when Robbie joined our group at the previous house. Sheila used to work (you know, I still can't fathom out exactly what this strange thing called work is that nearly all the humans seem to have to do at some time in their lives - it's certainly nothing that cats need to do; we can get along very well without it) in some big building in town and, apparently, one day this very affable and handsome bright ginger-and-white cat appeared seemingly from nowhere and set up camp outside the front entrance. Everyone that passed by patted him and spoke to him and gave him cat treats and bowls of milk, etc. At night the humans would take it in turns to provide him with a dinner - whether it was an 'own brand dinner' I didn't know, but I expect he was grateful for whatever he was given! It was obvious he had come from somewhere fairly close by and perhaps had fallen on bad times. At any rate, he had had the presence of mind to pack his kitty bag and turn up at this place full of humans where he knew he could perhaps obtain help. I have always admired him for that. It takes great courage for a little cat-sized person to think of doing such a thing. At any rate, this all went on for about three weeks, during which time the humans found out that he had originally lived in a nearby road of houses all used by very elderly humans. His own elderly human had passed away to wherever humans go and her relations did not want Robbie and turned him out into the streets - a good example of how some humans are NOT cat lovers! A humans' summer holiday weekend was approaching and everyone was worried about how Robbie would be fed. Nobody could offer him a home, but Sheila, who had originally thought that with having four cats already (me, Tansy, Lucky and Taro) they couldn't take on any more, just could not bear to see him abandoned. She had contacted two cat refuge places, but they had been full up and had advised her to get him 'put down' - another phrase I've never understood; what does it mean? It obviously means something really nasty because she was horrified and immediately made up her mind that he was coming home to join us! Firstly she took him to see Mr Kingdon, the vet, who gave him a clean bill of health, and then she borrowed a basket and arrived back home with him! At the time, her father lived in a little house - rather like Peter's motor machines have now - attached to the main house. Worried about how Robbie would get on with four strange cats, she decided that he would spend the first night with her father to get him accustomed to his new surroundings. I heard from Robbie later that he had been unable to sleep as he was so terrified at the awful wheezing, roaring sounds that Sheila's father made all night! Why is it male humans seem to make this unpleasant and unsociable noise when they sleep? You should be

93

quiet when you sleep. I do not admit to making any annoying sounds, just gentle purring, which is a nice, calming noise - quite hypnotic in its way and I believe humans find a cat's purring to be a real stress reliever. We were all very curious about what was going on in Sheila's father's living area, as we had seen her arrive there with this unknown cat hidden in the basket. It sounded all very suspicious to us and none of us could settle down that evening. However, the next afternoon we were all sitting either in the lounge or the strange oblong-shaped room that adjoined it with transparent walls and roof (a favourite place of we cats to sit in when it was sunny) when Sheila's father let Robbie make his own way through the lounge towards us. When I think of it now, he certainly had some bottle (but then, of course, we knew that from the way he had cleverly gone for help to Sheila's workplace). I don't know what Robbie must have been expecting upon seeing four strange cats of all shapes, sizes and colours, but - using the universal cats' slow-motion walk - he passed right amongst us and lay down under a chair in the transparent room. He then proceeded to ignore us totally, but I bet underneath he was saying, "Phew, glad that's over", to himself! Well, his low-key entrance rather took the wind out of our sails, so we did nothing either! I think the humans had expected fisticuffs and fur flying everywhere! Anyway, from that day on Robbie (well they never knew his real name, but they called him that after Sheila's boss's little pet dog - heaven knows why!) integrated into the family and we all lived happily together from then on.

1.15pm Time for lunch. Don't the hours just fly by when you are daydreaming or dozing? We, apart from Pandy, went into the kitchen and Sheila threw together some stuff for our meal. She obviously wasn't going to bother making much of a culinary effort today in the heat. I reckoned that she would be getting

Peter to fetch in something for their dinner later from the takeaway food place (for humans only, not cats) in the village. I ate a bit of lunch - even I wasn't particularly hungry today - and wandered into the dining room to my favourite place for my afternoon snooze. I had a most delightful scratch - you know, the type when you start off just suppressing a little itch, and then the more you carry on the more enjoyable it gets and you don't want to stop! I can tell you that it was not a flea causing my itch as the humans put drops on my neck every month which, for some inexplicable reason, keep those little devils right away from me. I expect it was a 'heat' itch! Anyway, reluctantly I stopped and fell asleep again.

4.00pm I woke up and began thinking about Robbie again. After he had been in our company for two or three weeks, the humans decided that it was time to let him out into the large garden that I described earlier. Well, for all his bravado, Robbie became a quivering wreck as he first surveyed the enormous expanse of green grass that surrounded the house! He simply sank down on his haunches, and, if he could have lifted his paws over both his eyes to blot out the terrifying sight, he would have! We couldn't understand it - we all loved the place and thought it was like a huge park full of attractions that any animal would have been happy in. It took about a week before he felt sufficiently confident to start to explore, but after that he became as used to it all as we were. He told me much later that he had spent the entire earlier part of his life in the house of the old lady human and had never been out of doors in all that time. He had spent his days either sitting on her lap or looking out of the window onto a small, dark street with no sign of any green grass. When he had first seen this strange stuff at our house covering everything as far as he could see, he had panicked. Well, I could understand him - when Tansy and I arrived as kittens we, too, had been somewhat amazed at this huge open area and, in fact, Sheila had made us wear infuriating harnesses and took us around initially on leads like dogs wear (we were too young at the time to understand how humiliating that was!) until we got used to it all. In retrospect she was right - we were so tiny that we might have lost our bearings and got hopelessly lost! Robbie was always cheerful, and such a friendly soul with a good word and a smile for everyone, and we all loved him, but he had some very bad luck whilst he lived with us. After about a year or two had gone by he developed something in one of his eyes - a kind of black patch that got larger as time went on and made his eye swell up. It really must have felt extremely uncomfortable, but he never complained. Mr Kingdon, the vet, kept one of his own eyes on it and eventually declared that unfortunately there was nothing for it but to have it removed. Sheila and Peter had an absolute fit at this, but Mr Kingdon assured them that Robbie would feel happier without it as it was now such an encumbrance to him. Also, he probably hadn't been able to see out of it for some time, he told them, and he could manage quite well with just the other eye, which was perfectly healthy. Nevertheless, the rest of us were very nervous and upset about it all but, typical of Robbie, when the day of his operation loomed he calmly sailed through and made no fuss whatsoever. Mr Kingdon did a very good bit of embroidery, closing up where the eye had been, and was most careful with Robbie's fur, making sure that he still looked handsome but with one eye shut as if he were permanently winking at everybody! It didn't detract from his appearance at all. Even Sheila cheered up as she saw that Robbie himself seemed quite unconcerned about it all. Mr Kingdon had cleverly bandaged one of his front paws up after the operation, so

Robbie spent the whole time wondering what had happened to his paw and trying - unsuccessfully - to undo the bandaging! This crafty trick kept his attention from his eye which, in truth, surely must have felt a bit odd. Anyway, all's well that ends well, as they say. Robbie continued enjoying life for several more years before he finally joined the others in their giant cat basket in the sky.

6.50pm Peter was home and he and Sheila had had a nice-smelling fish and chip supper which, as I'd surmised, he'd brought in on his way home. They did give me some nice bits of the fish and I also had a reasonable dinner of my own. We were all about to move into the lounge for our nightly sit down when we heard a whirring and banging sound from somewhere above the cooking area where there is a kind of pipe going up through the ceiling. They pricked up their ears - but as their ears are so small you couldn't notice any movement. Mine, on the other hand, were standing right up, as I could quite easily identify those sounds - a bird! How exciting, and inside the house too! Pandy, who was still outside lingering on the patio by the open back door, was also getting quite excited and was hopping up and down on the step, eager to see what was happening. The bird was now fluttering and squeaking - how lovely that sound is to a cat. Many moons now, I'm afraid, since I last caught one. Nowadays I am a birdwatcher not a catcher. Sheila was sure it was actually in the pipe and, although he wasn't sure about it, she finally persuaded Peter to dismantle it. This he managed to do, but no bird! Those words I do not like to hear were being said by both him and Sheila! But still we could all hear it flapping about. My mouth was watering and I expect Pandy's was too. I'm sure we could have winkled the bird out in no time. However, the humans decided to look in the space at the top of the house (somewhere I've never been able to get to and explore as yet) to see if the bird had somehow fallen down from there. Infuriatingly they closed the inner kitchen door so I was unable to follow them. Pandy and I then heard a bit of banging and then the sound of the window in the room above being opened. I went outside just in time to see Peter throw a starling out of the window. It was rather dishevelled and obviously a youngster - prime and tender as Pandy remarked - and it teetered tantalisingly on the edge of the low roof above us. We were both by this time on our hind legs waiting for this unexpected gift from heaven to float down to us, but - just our luck - suddenly it appeared to pull itself together and flew off to another high point on the roof. Well, what a bummer! We well missed out on that one! Oh well, it was obviously not to be. Pandy wandered off disappointed and I went inside again and found Sheila and Peter upstairs looking ruefully at a square hole he had had to cut into the surround of the pipe to extract the unlucky bird. Apparently it had fallen down not directly into the pipe but between that and its protective boxing.

8.15 - 11.00pm Well, we all sat in the lounge and I stretched out on Sheila's knee, thinking miserably of the starling treat I had just missed. She was going on at Peter about him having to make a hole in the wall and he was going on at her about making him unnecessarily dismantle the kitchen chimney - altogether, not a pair of happy bunnies! I put my sleep mode switch in the on position and left them to it!

11.15pm Bedtime.

Saturday:

8.45am The last day of the week had rolled round again and so I was coming to the end of my diary. Despite not much happening on the home front, the week seemed to have gone by quickly. It had been lovely and warm - perfect weather for we cats - and I had enjoyed looking back and remembering my past feline and canine friends and telling you about them. I hope you have enjoyed hearing about them too! Peter was busy carrying out his cleaning duties around my corner, and I was just about to eat my breakfast before I ventured outside once more.

9.10am I went out onto the patio and sniffed the air - nice and fresh and, again, it looked as if we were in for a hot day. I performed the usual early morning ritual of carrying out my private functions, followed by fur washing and whisker licking, and strolled back in. Sheila was loading another of her noisy machines with piles of their outer coverings, all types and colours. What a waste of her time! Why can't they be content with the one pale pink outfit they seem to wear underneath? Admittedly, neither she nor Peter look very good in just their underneath skins - perhaps that is why they are obsessed with covering themselves up all the time - but surely SO many different things are quite unnecessary. Likewise, if I go into their sleeping room I see hundreds of those things they, particularly Sheila, fit over their paws and I really can't see why they need to do this. Cats walk, run, climb and go anywhere needing nothing on their paws. Still, as I am continually noticing, humans just do not have the savvy of cats and waste their time and energy on being so disorganised - no wonder they get stressed up and shout out all those naughty words! Cats stay cool, calm and collected, plan their lives carefully and so come out on top every time! Easy-peasy when you know how, and I am a past master at all this, as readers of my last year's diary will already have discovered!

11.30am The humans had gone out and a line of their outer coverings was hanging out in the bright sunlight in the garden. Pandy had not yet made an appearance, so I stretched out on the nice, dry grass and prepared to enjoy the warmth flowing over me. Sleep was flowing over me too - what's new?!

1.30pm I awoke to see Pandy approaching. He has ears as sharp as an owl's and had heard the sound of Peter's motor machine returning. As usual, he dashed round the front of the house to get into the motor machine's home to see if any titbits were forthcoming. (Previous readers will know that Pandy has the perfect food scam. When Peter opens the flap in the side of the house so he can get the motor machine in, Pandy rushes round and hides under the other machine in there and, until Peter bribes him with something to eat, he refuses to budge. This works every time!) Sadly for Pandy, today Peter left his machine outside, so there were no bribes forthcoming!

1.40pm I went indoors to greet Sheila and Peter and, more importantly, to see if anything had been put out for my lunch. They seemed to be decanting a lot of packages, bottles and cans, etc., onto the kitchen table and I realised they had been doing their big weekly food shop. Yes, thankfully, I could see a stack of tins and packets of my food as well. Good. I noticed that there were no 'own brand' items in the pile today - Peter had obviously taken good notice of my strong hint earlier in the week! Sheila busied herself putting things away and then inserted a couple of items into yet another of her infernal machines. This one to me looks like a smaller version of the big silver box they are glued to each night in the lounge, but somehow quite delicious smells of food emanate from it after a few minutes. Miraculous, and I have to admit that even a clever clogs like me cannot understand just how that particular machine works!

1.50pm Everyone was now outside in the garden again and the humans were eating some things she'd taken from the machine and said were called 'hot dogs'! How strange - they looked nothing like dogs to me. I've never heard of them - are there 'hot cats' as well? Anyway, they kept dropping me pieces down and I must say they were very tasty. Looked more like sausages than dogs to me! I've always liked a bit of sausage almost as much as a bit of cheese. Pandy winkled out a few bits from Peter too! We all sat happily drinking in the sun for a while - cats and humans in harmony.

3.30pm The sun by now was really quite hot and I retired under a stone shelter in the garden half asleep again but with one eye on the others. Peter had removed the top of his outer coverings and was exposing his pale pink top half to the sun, but by the end of the afternoon the pale pink had become a browny-pink and his face had turned equally brown but his snout was rather a bright red! Sheila, who did not remove all her top outer covering but did put on those unflattering shorts, was quickly turning a nasty shade of red. Rather unattractive if you ask me - fur comes in much nicer colour schemes. Still, each to his own, as they say! Perhaps they thought being in the sun and turning a few shades darker made them more attractive - exactly to whom I couldn't imagine!

6.00pm Well, we were all a bit tired after the heat of the day, so Pandy limped off to his own home, hoping for an early dinner there so that he could then come back here and tell his usual 'porkies' to my humans that his own humans never fed him, etc. They always fall for this line, so he knows he's on to a winner and will be given my leftovers as his second dinner. It is always polite to leave a bit on your plate - I rarely clean mine up completely unless I've been eating some of the luxury stuff that Lois brings. Food, food, food - that's all Pandy ever seems to think about!

Mind you, he is a bit on the thin side despite all that he crams down. I have always had to watch what I eat as I never wanted to turn out to be a really fat cat. Just to be a nice-sized, cuddly, fat cat was my aim and I've always made sure I've stayed that way.

6.30pm We all sat outside eating our dinner, although none of us was particularly hungry, it being so hot. Sheila and Peter lolled in their seats and I lay down on the flower bed with the slate chippings that I find so comfy. Once more in a drowsy state, I decided to see if I could remember one last amusing event to put into my diary.

7.15pm Oh yes, I could remember something that I hope will make you smile. It still makes me do so after all these years! We were all in the garden of the other house and it was a super day like today had been. Tansy and Lucky were sitting at the edge of the pond, peering out to see if there was any movement to indicate that the fish were nearby or maybe any of the other creatures we used to get in there - newts, frogs, dragonflies, water boatmen, etc. Suddenly Lucky spotted a couple of eels approaching. Now, occasionally these strange things - I really don't know if they are fish or animals - did visit. They came from a nearby stream in the next-door field I think. Anyway, we cats had caught an eel from time to time - very difficult I might say. They are so slippery and slimy that even with our sharp claws we've not often been able to hold on to one. Lucky and Tansy jumped up and Taro and myself, hearing Lucky's cry of excitement, also ran towards the pond. The humans never moved, of course, as they did not understand what Lucky was shouting about. The two eels continued on their way towards where we were waiting, two V-shaped ripples on the pond indicating that they were just easily swimming along. Lucky and Tansy were shoulder to shoulder now, ready to pounce as soon as the eels came within reaching distance. We were all in that mixed state of happy anticipation and tension - the lovely moment when you feel that a mouse or bird or, indeed, an eel is about to be caught! But disaster was about to befall us - Hennessy! Out of nowhere he came lumbering towards the pond edge. He had heard the commotion and, never one to sit quietly in the background, was eager to see what was happening. Up he came and in his usual clumsy manner collided with the group of watching cats, knocking Tansy, Lucky and Taro right into the water - NOT me, I'm thankful to say, as I was slightly to one side.

Splish, splosh - thanks Hennessey!

Well - splash, splash, splash - in they toppled. The eels immediately took to their heels (I presume eels have heels! Sounds as if they should, doesn't it? Eel heels!) and Sheila and Peter did then dash over to see what was happening. Afterwards they always said they'd wished they'd had one of those little machines they use to take moving pictures handy (another humans' device that I can't get my head around). Lucky immediately swam to the bank, shook himself and climbed back out. Taro followed - very upset and tearful that his beautiful, haute couture, fur catsuit was now all wet and muddy! (He took several days to get over this hiccup to his usual sartorial elegance!) But, worst of all, little Tansy, panicking, paddled wildly and instead of heading towards the bank she went in the opposite direction and ended up on the island! Of course, when she hauled herself up, she realised that she was now marooned in the middle of the pond! Immediately she started caterwauling at the top of her voice, very agitated indeed. We sat stunned, not knowing what to do. Hennessy was trying to apologise to all and sundry (how hopeless was that dog?), but that wasn't going to help Tansy in her situation. So, Peter to the rescue! It was not as easy as it seemed. The pond was not very deep at the edge, about 50cm, but it gradually got deeper towards the middle and the island, where it was well over a metre in depth. The bottom of the pond was thick with sludgy mud and, immediately Peter stepped in, his paws sank right in and he could barely take a step forward. However, he crept on gingerly even though he had soon sunk almost up to the tops of his legs. Sheila was rushing to and fro in her usual helpless kind of way and produced some of those paw coverings they sometimes wear - bright green rubber boots. She, too, got into the water but her boots got firmly embedded in the mud and she stuck fast! Peter was gradually making his way to the island and, some few minutes later, he managed to reach it and pick up Tansy, who was shivering and mewing most piteously. Sheila had to haul herself out of her boots - leaving them embedded in the mud - and scramble back onto the bank herself. I had to hide a smile. Now her legs were all brown, something all her sitting in the sun hadn't achieved! Silly human that she is - why did she get in in the first place? She's never any help in an emergency! Well, eventually everyone was out and dried off. Tansy was petted and comforted and Hennessy was told off once again! Not that any of his tellings-off had ever had any effect but, as I remarked earlier, despite all his clumsiness everyone loved him, so he was never in the dog house for long! All was well in the end and it was a rather funny episode, but it could have turned out to be a disaster if Peter had been unable to reach Tansy.

9.30pm Indoors we trooped and sat down in the lounge, the humans box-watching again! The week was just about over and my diary complete. On balance, I have had yet another peaceful, happy and healthy year living with my human family and I look forward to the next one and several more too. I probably won't put paw to paper again, though. Two diaries is enough for any cat to write! I do hope you, dear reader, have enjoyed another insight into my life. As you will realise, a cat will never fully understand humans and their strange habits, and humans will certainly never understand we cats and our views on life. However, it is nice to know that, in general, we can all live together harmoniously, isn't it? Give and take and quite often compromise, that's the secret of interactive living! Well, time is getting on and soon bedtime will come round again before yet another day dawns for me!

11.30pm Well, that's it - goodnight and goodbye! Truffles over and out!

THE ENCORE

CATCH UP ...

Well, hello again humans! Yes, I know I said at the end of my last diary that I thought I would not put paw to paper again! However, many of you apparently pleaded with my carer, Sheila, saying that you wanted to hear from me again, so she has persuaded me - with the help of some extra portions of chicken and sardines, etc. - to put on my thinking cap once more and try to remember some more tales of my long life and also to catalogue more of my philosophies on your strange human ways!

For those of you who have not read my two previous little diaries about me and my human carers, Sheila and Peter, please do go out and get them because then you will know much more about my background and what has gone on during the past eighteen/nearly nineteen years of my life. It is now spring 2007 and the current feline character list has altered somewhat in the last six months, so I will let you know what has happened.

Firstly, I am quite sad and bewildered because my good friend (although we've always had a love/hate relationship!) Pandy, from next door, seems to have vanished. I last saw him back in October and he seemed fine then. He was in my humans' place where their motor machines sleep and he was also sleeping in a little bed they kept for him in there. I then saw him making his usual slow way around the back garden path but after that - nothing! Though I looked out of the patio doors every day for weeks after, still nothing. How strange. I can't understand it. I did see that a couple of days later my humans were very quiet and Sheila had those funny drops of water coming out of her eyes. I heard them saying something about Pandy having had several strokes. Well, what does that mean? Nothing to get upset about I would have thought - strokes are nice things, like pats, and I enjoy plenty of them. Pandy enjoyed them too, I'm sure.

Then the neighbours came in and told them that Pandy was now under a rose tree - water was dropping out of their eyes too - another peculiar thing! I know cats like to climb up trees, but I can't see how they could get under a tree! So, it baffles me. The humans seem okay now, but I still can't quite get my head around it all and I still wonder about my old friend ...

Anyway, there have been a lot of changes next door since Pandy vanished. I told you in my last book about Milly and Lily, the two young glamour pusses, who joined the family earlier in the year. One of our local tomcat gigolos, Bob, had his evil way with both of them (at different times, I might say, not a threesome!) and the consequence was that they both had families of beautiful kittens. Milly was first and she produced several, but her humans gave them all away except one, called Alfie, who is a very handsome lad, I must say - a long-furred silvery-fawn tabby. It's perhaps fortunate that I am now at my advanced age and not a youngster myself or I may have been tempted to alter my virginal way of life!

A few months later it was Lily's turn. She produced several handsome babies and her humans kept two: Chip, who is the image of her, with beautifully marked, long silver fur; and Bob Junior, who is the image of his rapist dad, i.e. semi-long black fur with white trim. When they were only a few months old, though, sadly Lily also disappeared. What bad luck that family next door has had with their feline companions. I believe poor Lily was knocked down by some other human's motor machine. Lethal those things are for we cats. I have always maintained a very wide berth from the roadway outside our house. Another cat from next door, confusingly also called Bob, was knocked over the previous year in the same manner. Why do you humans worship these horrible, hateful motor machines that are such a danger to cats and dogs? Peter spends half his time fussing over his two machines, cleaning them just so they can get dirty all over again. What a waste of time!

Then some time later that little hussy, Milly, did it again. Yes, Bob the rapist got her in his paws once more! This time the result was Ernie and Molly, one black with white trim like his dad and the other more black with just a smattering of white on the chest. After this debacle, Milly was taken to the local vet and 'seen to' and also Alfie, Chip and Bob Junior suffered the same fate - whatever that means - but I heard their humans telling ours that certainly NO more kittens were going to be allowed in their home! I daresay Mollie and Ernie will be 'seen to' in due course, ensuring that the neighbours' collective total of six cats will remain at that level. Since they also have a hooligan of a West Highland terrier called Oscar and a tiny little shih-tzu puppy called Princess, I think they must think they are running a cattery or a kennel next door. As for me, well, I like to be the kingpin (or queenpin in my case) of the household and be the only feline to give orders to my carers. I wouldn't like to have to contend with other cats trying to usurp my authority!

Well, that's you up to date with the changes. The rest of my past feline pals - Coco, Sasha, Taro, Lucky, Tansy, Robbie - and let's not forget the two stupid dogs, Lady and Hennessy and that awful macaw parrot, Geronimo - will turn up again in some more of my recollections of events now long gone. I thought after two books of memories I wouldn't be able to remember many more funny things to tell you, but I will dig deep and see how we go! I am glad to have all my faculties still - the 'Truffles dementia years' have yet to come! However, before I start this latest diary, it's time for a good, long sleep to refresh those little grey cells, so see you 'd'reckly' (as they say in here in Cornwall).

My old mate, Pandy

SUNDAY

7.30am: I was deeply asleep in my comfy bed when I was rudely awakened by Peter coming noisily into the kitchen. I know he clumps about on purpose just to wake me up. At least on weekends I do have an extra hour's sleep time before he disturbs me. With an air of hope he then expects me to jump up, greet him fulsomely and rush out into the garden to carry out my ablutions as per his timetable. Dream on, Peter! He has never succeeded in this plan - even in the warm days of summer - and certainly now that it is only April and freezing cold there is absolutely no way I am going to go outside the house and, worse still, expose my derrière to the icy blasts, so I glared up at him, turned round in bed and pointedly ignored him. I heard him muttering those words that well-bred pussies do not wish to hear under his breath, but then the sound of his sweeping up the granules of cat litter from around my litter igloo made me give a contented smile to myself. Peter wasn't smiling - his lips were pursed - but at least he was still performing his required duties. Nobody gets away

112

with interfering with MY timetable. I decided I would let him tidy it all up and then leave it a little while before making my way into the igloo, performing and so messing up all the litter again. Kittenish I know, but one of the things I do enjoy in life is the feeling of power I have over my humans in that, apart from the fact that I require pristine litter at all times to await any sudden lavatorial urges that might overcome me, I know they also like to see the litter clean, as for some reason they don't appear to like the natural odours that I leave behind me after each use. Still, I will draw a veil over my toilet arrangements now, as I don't suppose, dear reader, that you want to spend any more time musing on that rather intimate subject!

7.40am: Peter was pouring water into that gadget that seems to turn it into the brown frothy stuff he and Sheila like to drink and he then sat down and proceeded to eat his breakfast - a bowl of humans' crunchies. I bet they're not as tasty as my cat crunchies, flavoured with salmon or chicken or shrimp, etc. I continued to relax in my bed, keeping one eye on him so that once he was comfortably settled and reading his newspaper I could get up and demand that I was given my breakfast too.

7.45am: I stretched, got out of bed and had a drink of nice fresh water from my personal drinking machine. This high-tech system was a present they brought home after visiting a big cat show in Birmingham last autumn. I love it! They have all these electric gadgets themselves in the kitchen and at last I have one too. It looks like an ordinary water bowl, but somehow a fountain of water runs into to it continuously so that the water stays nice and fresh, and I like catching the bubbles it produces on my tongue as I am lapping. I think it will be a godsend in the summer if the weather is as hot as it was last year - I heard Peter telling Sheila that ice cubes can be put into it somewhere to keep the water lovely and cool.

7.47am: Peter, realising that I was now up and about, produced my breakfast bowl and placed it on my mat. I strolled up to it and sniffed suspiciously - what was it this time? Not leftovers from last night's tin I hoped. I hadn't been too keen on that - some kind of mushy fish and meat mix. I feared it was an 'own brand' kind of tin, as sometimes they try to save money (whatever that is!) and get these tins instead of the branded ones I really like. However, I could breathe again - it was a fresh meal of prawns in jelly, so I gobbled it up quite quickly. Mmm, it was actually very good!

7.55am: Breakfast finished, it was time for whisker licking, and so I returned to bed to complete this procedure. I took my time and then decided to inspect the newly cleaned-out litter igloo and give it the seal of my satisfaction - ah, that felt good! Then I returned once more to bed for the derrière licking process. That's something all cats like to do - keep their nether regions scrupulously clean. Upon completion of this ritual, I gazed up at Peter as, according to my timetable, it was time for him to give me my weekly fur-do. I have to admit that he is very good at combing and arranging my fur and keeping my coat glossy - I've never needed to go to one of those pet grooming parlours. Next door they spend a fortune on having their dogs crimped and curled!

8.30am: All the early morning routine, plus fur-do, now out of the way, with Peter happily (I hoped) re-cleaning my litter igloo, I made my way into the dining room to recline on my personal mat located just inside the transparent patio doors through which a bit of watery sun was now streaming. Though I could see it looked very chilly outside with strange white tips to the grass and plants, that jolly fellow in the yellow hat up in the sky was doing his bit to keep me warm, his rays penetrating the aforesaid doors. I know I am uncommonly clever for a cat, but I have to admit quite candidly that I cannot get my head around the human miracle of these see-through doors and panels in the walls of houses. Marvellous and so convenient - I can watch what's going on outside and if any strange cats appear and look in at me I can growl, hiss and swear at them to my heart's content in the knowledge that they can't touch me! I do this quite often, as there are several cats who dare to intrude into my garden. As I hardly go outdoors myself now, except when the weather is really warm, it annoys me to see these trespassers. However, a few well-chosen swear words (which I learned from Geronimo, the foul-mouthed macaw who used to live with us some years back) usually send them packing!

11.00am: I had fallen into a doze – so what's new? However, I suddenly became wide awake, as I could see young Alfie from next door standing outside and peering in at me. He was pawing at the see-through panel and making it quite smeary with the mud from under his paws, so I drew myself up to my full height and proceeded to give him a few well-chosen hisses and growls. He backed off immediately, turned tail and disappeared back over the wall into next door's garden. Rightly so - he should keep to his own garden! Mine is not a pleasure park for other felines, it is strictly reserved 'pour moi'. Having woken up fully now, I strolled out into the hall to see what the humans were up to. From the noises coming from the motor machines' quarters, Peter was busy cleaning them yet again. What a futile task, as I said earlier, as immediately he takes them out for exercise they get all dirty again. Still, cleaning them once a week and pottering around in their house seem to keep him happy - strange things seem to keep humans happy.

11.30am: Going upstairs and into the study, I climbed onto my favourite chair. If I am not on the rug in the dining room by the patio, this is my next best place in the house. Sheila was at her computer - another human gadget that I cannot altogether get my head around - where she seems to spend most of her time nowadays. She flutters her paws as if playing the piano and all sorts of colourful images appear on a square panel above it. Sometimes I look at these in absolute fascination and at other times it is just boring as all I can see are lines and lines of print - text she calls it I believe. Still, I mustn't criticise because it is on this machine that she slaves away writing down my diaries for me - and for you - to read. So, understand it or not, it is a godsend for both of us.

2.00pm: Sheila had disappeared downstairs to prepare a midday meal for herself and Peter, and I had been having a sleeping session – I have to get in my 22 hours' sleep per day, you know! I woke up, had a stretch and glanced out through the transparent panel in the outside wall - the sun was still very bright. I have a good view from here of the garden and trees and also of the many birds that congregate on the branches. Temptingly good they look too (the birds I mean, not the trees!) but I'm afraid nowadays that's all I can do - look not catch. Although I am pretty fit and still have the odd mad dash up and down the stairs, etc., I have to admit that the edge I had over the birds in terms of both speed and surprise has diminished now. No doubt Alfie and his mates keep the bird population under control though! It is nice being high up, and that reminds me of one of my predecessors - Coco - so I will make myself comfortable and tell you what happened to her once long ago.

3.30pm: Whoops - I fell asleep again! Anyway, Coco used to live with Peter and Sheila quite a while before I came on the scene.

Previous readers of my diaries will have heard all about their past felines. Lucky, the pale ginger and white cat, who was always my best pal when we lived at our previous place in Cornwall - the one with the large garden and lake - and who had known Coco, told me all about her. She had lived with the family when they had a house by the sea before moving to the country location. All the houses in that particular seaside village were very old and two or three storeys in height, most of them having no lovely garden but small, hemmed-in courtyards instead. One day Peter was at work and Sheila had taken a 'day off work', whatever that word 'work' conjures up - yet another thing that seems common to humans but not to we cats and, again, something I'm not too clear about. At any rate, cats certainly do NOT work, so I wonder why it is that humans seem to set such store by it? From what I overhear, 'work' seems to turn into 'money', but again that is something I don't understand, and as cats certainly don't need either work or money to survive, well, WHY do humans feel the need? Oh well, another anomaly between us!

But, as usual, I digress ... So, as I said, Sheila was at home alone when she heard loud howls and cries coming from the back courtyard of next door's house. Upon investigation she could see Coco stranded on the top of a high, narrow wall, seemingly unable to move in any direction. She rushed out and Coco's screams rose several octaves higher on seeing her. By this time, said Lucky, who at the time was comfortably curled up on a warm flower bed in the courtyard surveying the proceedings with great interest, the howls were so loud that it was a wonder the whole street hadn't complained.

Sheila, being totally unpractical and unable to climb like we cats, could not reach Coco, so she told Coco to hang on in there and quieten down (some chance!) and rushed over the road to the local meeting place where the humans and their friends gathered to talk over stuff and drink copious amounts of lurid-coloured liquids that either seemed to turn them into laughing, silly idiots or, on occasions, get some of them all fired up and stroppy. Again, if humans only had the sense of cats and stuck to pure water or pure milk, no personality changes would occur and everyone would remain serene and happy! Fortunately for Coco, a strapping male human, whom Sheila apparently knew, was in this place having a drink and he had a ladder (not on him at the time, needless to say!) so he came to the rescue. This event apparently caused much mirth in the establishment - I don't know why humans always find it so funny when cats get stuck up on high walls or trees! Nobody was at home in the house next door, so the chap - John was his name - put his ladder up against the wall and with the deftness of a professional cat burglar (excuse the pun!) soon climbed up, grabbed Coco and brought her down safely to ground level once again.

So the situation was resolved and everyone was happy, until a short time later a couple of fierce-looking humans in identical dark blue uniforms arrived and began banging on Sheila's front door. Apparently some do-gooder human had reported seeing a shifty-looking man climbing over her neighbour's wall and they asked her if she knew anything about it or if she had seen anything. Well, the 'shifty-looking man', who was at that moment drinking a cup of the frothy stuff humans drink in Sheila's kitchen, had to come clean and admit that he had been rescuing her cat! The fierce men suddenly became much less fierce and started laughing, and then everyone was laughing and, as Lucky said, the story of Coco's rescue became the talking point for all the humans in the drinking place for weeks and poor John never lived it down!

Coco stranded

5.45pm: My tummy was rumbling, so I sauntered into the kitchen to see what delights were nestling in my dinner bowl. However, a rather unpleasant smell invaded my nostrils as I neared it and the food inside looked an extremely distasteful fawn/pinkish colour. I examined it in more detail - ugh! As you humans are prone to say - it looked like something the cat had dragged in! Well, I can tell you, this cat would certainly not have lifted a paw to bring that stuff in! Sheila was obviously trying to fob me off again with an 'own brand' cat food. She does this from time to time - trying to save money so she says - but I was not having it; no, I was certainly NOT having it! I was immediately thrown into a bad temper - the more so because I had been feeling rather hungry - and so I stalked into the main part of the kitchen where madam was standing in front of their cooking machine and lifting something out that really did smell good! That's right, I thought churlishly, feed yourselves with something delicious and let poor old Truffles have the dregs.

I rubbed rather harshly around Sheila's legs so that she looked down, and when our eyes met I let rip with some angry meows that clearly she understood right away because she very guiltily said, "Oh, Truffles, I'm sorry - I forgot to get your special tins today and had to give you one of the cheap spares I keep in case of an emergency." Sorry my paw, I thought! If I hadn't made a fuss she would never have said a thing and just hoped that I wouldn't notice! Anyway, I continued to voice my disapproval and a few minutes later she put some of their own dinner into a bowl for me - so, a result! Mollified, I ate it right up and then, sated, I retired to lie on my sofa bed. I was still feeling cross and resolved to keep my eye on Sheila, as I will not be fobbed off with inferior food - how do you think I have survived to be so healthy at nearly nineteen of your human years? Certainly not by eating rubbish! By ensuring I only have the best of everything, of course! Finally I dozed off. I never let myself get stressed for too long over any annoying event - life just isn't worth it.

8.45pm: My, my - look at the time! It does fly when you are enjoying yourself or asleep, doesn't it? As I've said repeatedly, I aim to sleep for 22 hours out of 24 and usually manage to achieve this!

9.30pm: I was now sitting on Sheila's knee whilst she and Peter transfixed their gaze on the large, silver, oblong box in the corner of the lounge (another of their pointless pastimes) and I recalled another mountaineering escapade involving Taro when he was younger. Taro called himself a Birman and was the 'aristocat' of the family. He wore a haute couture fur cat suit that was cream with a seal-coloured trim and he was immensely proud of his outfit and made every effort never to get himself dirty. I always thought he was rather a sissy myself! To protect his precious fur he always tried to make sure he was well out of the way of Hennessy the St Bernard, who was very clumsy and tended to drool everywhere. Readers of my previous two diaries will know that poor Taro didn't always manage this, as Hennessy caused him to have two accidents, one of which involved his falling down the stairs and the other causing him to tumble into our muddy pond! Taro was far more upset about falling into the pond and getting covered in mud than he was about falling down the stairs and fracturing one of his legs! Anyway, as usual, dear reader, I digress, so I will get back to Taro and his climbing mishap. Whilst the family was still living in the seaside village where Coco got stuck on a neighbour's wall, Taro one day also decided - somewhat out of character, I imagine - to be adventurous. He clambered out of the high-walled courtyard and onto the roof next door, and from that roof jumped over to the next roof, and so on, until he was about five or six houses away and found himself marooned on the top of a very high wall with no way forward and no way back. Panic then set in but, unlike Coco, he didn't think of screaming for help. So he just sat there, digging his paws in, and waited to be rescued.

Fortunately for Taro, Sheila was contacted by a neighbour who had spotted him on her roof and had then watched his progress with some amusement until she saw that he was, indeed, trapped on the high wall. Sheila and the neighbour then went to see the elderly humans who owned the house with the high wall and they all went up to the highest room in the house to try to persuade Taro to jump in through the window. After much coaxing and brandishing of titbits, Taro eventually regained his bottle and, after a few moments of teetering on the edge, in a death-defying leap he bounded in through the window without checking where he would actually be able to land. All sensible cats plan a landing spot in advance of a jump and, as you humans will know, we generally land comfortably and correctly upright on all four paws. Taro, however, landed with an enormous, jangly crash on a weird contraption that I believe is called a piano! Apparently the elderly human who owned the house used to be a concert performer and this piano was now her pride and joy and was kept in a designated 'music room' and used for special occasions to entertain other human devotees of human-type music. I must say at this point that cats do not share humans' taste in music! We much prefer to listen to caterwauling from our own kind - a group of two or three of we cats sitting on a wall together creating cat music in unison is heaven to my ears, but I notice that very few humans seem to appreciate our feline musical tastes! Lucky once told me that he was practising a duet with Tansy one evening and somebody chucked a load of water over him! Still, each to his own, I suppose ...

The elderly human was not at all pleased about Taro landing heavily on a strip of an assortment of small, black and white, oblong shapes that ran along the side of the piano and was even more cross when he ran back along them once more when he had regained his equilibrium! Some pretty ghastly - and certainly not harmonious - noises emerged from her wonderful piano as he did this, but Sheila managed to grab him and then proceeded to calm both Taro and the old lady down. When she told Peter later about the adventure, she was hard pressed to keep a straight face as she related the story of Taro's crash-landing on the precious piano!

11.10pm: Time for bed - Sheila pushed me off her knees, so I wandered back into the kitchen, had a refreshing drink and a nice pre-bedtime scratch, and then went into sleep mode. Another day would soon be dawning!

Not so harmonious a drop for Taro!

MONDAY

6.40am: Well, I could tell it was a human's 'working day' because in came Peter, noisy as ever, waking me up at some ridiculous hour just because HE had to be up! How unfair! He smacked down my food dish on the mat and obviously expected me to rush straight over and gobble up what delicious delicacies it contained. No chance! Instead, I took my time and approached it at a dead slow pace. Well, I am not a puppet and I am certainly not going to be controlled by any human and ordered what I must do and what I must not do, nor when I must do it! That would be totally alien to feline policy! Much as we may love our human carers - and I most certainly love my two - cats should never fawn on them like dogs do or make themselves over-subservient at any time. Feline dignity must always be upheld and humans must understand their place in the pecking order and that they are not on a par with we cats, but always just under. That is the way to get the best out of life from one's human carers - trust me, after nearly nineteen years I KNOW this!

Anyway, I digress once more! I eventually arrived at my dish and inspected the contents. Not too bad, so I did eat some of it, after which it was the usual morning routine of whisker licking and fur washing, which I'm sure you don't particularly want to hear about yet again as I've already regaled you above with the details of my toilette and I've also described it all at length in my previous diaries!

8.00am: I could see through the window in my personal cat flap that Chip and Alfie from next door were both sitting on the adjoining wall eyeing up the sparrows and blue tits that were feeding on little sacks of bird food that Sheila and Peter hang out for them on a convenient bush. I take exception to their harassing MY birds in MY garden - why can't they look at the ones in their own garden? I have never been keen on letting other cats into my garden - Pandy was about the one exception - and I like to do my own harassing of the birds that dare to visit here. As far as birds are concerned nowadays, live and let live I say. At my advanced age, I am not going to waste my energies on a scrawny sparrow. Yes, I've had my moments in the past and there have been plenty of notches on my collar relating to bird conquests, but that was in my youth and it is a phase that all cats go through. We can't change our instincts. I know that some humans hold this against us, but it is part of cat psychology, an inborn instinct, and not open to change. Anyway, I glared through the cat flap at the other two cats.

8.20am: Oh dear, I am in BIG trouble now with Peter! A few minutes ago, not only Chip and Alfie but also Ernie, Molly and Bob Jnr from next door all arrived in a gang directly outside the cat flap. Alfie had spotted me staring at him and Chip on the wall, and must have taken offence. He rallied his troops and they with one accord advanced on the cat flap, deciding that they would retaliate and start staring in at ME! Well, I was suddenly overwhelmed with rage at this and, hurling decorum to the winds, I flung myself at the flap, shouting abuse - I even shocked myself! Unfortunately the cat flap window wasn't equal to my weight and a violent crack ensued, whereupon it caved outward, scattering the onlooking group of cats! Peter, who was reading his newspaper at the time and hadn't noticed the build-up of feline tensions around him, immediately jumped up, yelling blue murder at me. Pandemonium ensued! The other cats beat a hasty retreat and I was left, now looking suitably shamefaced, to face the music. I was immediately apologetic; I didn't know what had come over me. I'm not normally ruffled and usually I am the soul of discretion and act at all times with total dignity as befits my age and my celebrity status in the cat writers' world. Oh dear, oh dear, I had well and truly blotted my copybook this time. I slunk back into my bed without a further murmur.

8.45am: Peter was inspecting the cracked cat flap and saying those human words that cats and other small mammals do not like to hear. He then proceeded to repair the flap with white sticky tape, which - inconveniently for me - totally blocked my view through it. He was still muttering under his breath for several minutes following the incident. I remained still and silent, trying to blend into the background of my furry upholstered bed.

9.00am: Sheila arrived downstairs - she had still been in her own comfy bed during the excitement. She couldn't believe what had happened! However, she immediately took my side (well, I knew she would - she is, after all, my staunch ally at all times and is really my favourite of my two carers - sorry Peter!) She and Peter 'had words', as you humans say, but she was maintaining that I was a marvel to have stood up to no less than five cats surrounding my cat flap - particularly at my age! However, she did then start grumbling that they would have to fork out for a new cat flap. Of course, I've always had a deluxe, top-of-the-range cat flap - nothing but the best for me - so I admit I was sorry for them at this point. These cat flaps and other paraphernalia they buy for me do seem to cost of lot of human money - the stuff you all seem to set so much store by - and I know that my humans don't seem to want to spend it 'unnecessarily', so I did feel rather guilty that my rash actions had caused them trouble. Still, how was I to know that the wretched flap would break - surely I am not THAT heavy?! I still remained quiet and eventually Peter went into the part of the house where his motor machines live and returned with a spare flap that he had, apparently, kept for such an occasion as this when they updated my previous cat flap for a newer model. Luckily the old flap fitted, so things resumed an air of calm again and both Sheila and Peter were happy that they wouldn't have to buy a new cat flap after all. Phew, I could breathe again ...

Whoops!

10.30am: I crept quietly upstairs, as I thought I had best keep out of the way for a few hours, so I ended up in Sheila's study, sitting on my favourite chair. I soon felt drowsy, so turned on my sleep switch ...

1.00pm: I was suddenly jerked awake by the sound of a horrendously loud fanfare signalling that someone was at the front door. The hall below seemed to be full of humans all speaking at the same time, but on peering through the banisters I could see that there were only two others plus Sheila and Peter. I didn't recognise their two friends, but no matter, as almost immediately all four of them went out. Peace reigned, so I decided to make my way downstairs and see if any lunch had been left out for me. After the debacle earlier, I was a little worried that they might not have put anything out for me. Since I had been upstairs, nobody had been in even to look at me, so I assumed I was still in their bad books. However, on arrival at my corner in the kitchen I found some tasty crunchies and some pieces of chopped beef awaiting me in my bowl, so I soon made short work of them. Thank heavens my humans don't carry grievances for very long!

1.30pm: The cat flap now mended, I made my way through it into the garden. The sun was now shining and I sniffed the air appreciatively - mmm, lovely - the scent of the spring flowers was sweet and there was no scent of invading cats either! My neighbours had, no doubt, taken the hint that I do NOT like being spied on and perhaps they would remain in their own garden for a while now. I strolled around and then found a nice sunny patch on the patio. I lay there, warmed by the sunlight, and started to think about the past.

When we had Hennessy the St Bernard dog in our family at our previous house, he and I quite often used to lie in the sun together. Despite his thick fur and his breed's reputation for enjoying snowy and cold weather, he used to tell me that he liked relaxing in the heat best. Just as well really, because Cornwall is not well known for snow! Trouble was, Hennessy drooled so - there we would be, quite happily lying there, me set comfortably between his huge front paws, when all of a sudden, splash, a great dollop of slobber would land on my head! Ugh! I would then have to start washing my face and head furiously, with Hennessy apologising most profusely. He would try to make recompense by shaking his 'chops' from side to side to endeavour to get rid of the excess slobber, but that only made things worse and I would get showered again!

Hennessy was such a clumsy and stupid dog, but he was always very remorseful to we cats so we hadn't the heart to be too cross with him. We just got sick of continually having to wash our fur off when he was around! I remember that, several months after Hennessy had gone to that big dog basket in the sky, Sheila was in the kitchen and noticed dried blobs of his slobber right up on the ceiling! If he was ever heard drinking, she would rush into the kitchen and try to dry his 'chops' off with a rag before he shook his great head and sprayed water and slobber all round the room! Obviously on this occasion she must have missed her cue, hence the slobber marks on the ceiling! Oh well, sorry if I've made you feel queasy!

3.15pm: I was still lying comfortably on the patio and got to thinking again about Hennessy. Sheila and Peter had had him since he was six weeks old - and at that age he was much the same size as I am. When fully grown he was a giant and quite a handful to look after, I understand. He was, in fact, not a disobedient animal, though nobody could call him well trained exactly as he, like most dogs, was never so crafty or sharp as we cats, just rather dim we thought. Other dogs of smaller proportions used to think he was the 'Incredible Hulk' as he ambled along and many shied away from him, though the bolder ones, particularly small terriers and the like, would sometimes rush at him and attack his ankles in an attempt to prove that they were fierce and unafraid. Whilst placidly withstanding these pathetic assaults, dear old Hennessy would merely wag his feathery tail and let them get on with it, before gently nudging them or toppling them out of the way - a thoroughly humiliating experience for them, which brought them down a peg or two and took the cockiness out of them!

I recall Sheila telling some friends once that they had the most trouble on visits to the vet. As soon as they walked into the waiting room, all the other dogs there would immediately launch into a cacophony of barking, so to keep the peace they usually had to wait outside with him until it was their turn. On one occasion when they were called in, Hennessy rushed right through the middle of the room, with Sheila hanging horizontally onto the lead behind him, and crashed straight into the vet's consulting room, knocking the examination table to the ground! Fortunately the vet himself remained upright, but there was pure chaos for several moments. Readers of my previous books will know that poor, lovable, clumsy Hennessy caused plenty of chaos throughout his life, but Sheila and Peter always said they loved him to bits (as I guess we all did really), and whatever scrapes he got himself in he was always forgiven in the end.

Lucky told me that once, whilst Sheila and Hennessy were out walking, a stranger approached them and said she was from Switzerland where St Bernard dogs originated from. As a cat, I've never heard of this place Switzerland, but I don't believe it is anywhere in Cornwall. However, to continue, this lady human told Hennessy how beautiful he was (what a crawler!) and that she would send him a proper St Bernard's barrel to wear around his neck. True to her word, a few weeks later a beautiful handmade wooden barrel was delivered, decorated with painted flowers that were apparently native to this place, Switzerland, and there was even a brass tap on the front of the barrel. All this clipped onto Hennessy's collar and he proudly wore it on special occasions when he was out, always attracting a crowd of onlookers when he did so.

5.00pm: Well, I must have dozed off yet again! There's nothing wrong with that anyway - as a cat approaching her twilight years, that's how I conserve my energy, which, together with my insistence on top-quality food and total attention to my every whim from my dedicated human carers, is how I am living proof of a healthy cat! Well, this healthy cat, now suitably refreshed, looked around and spotted those cheeky little youngsters from next door - the latest of the clan, Chip, Molly and Ernie, were sitting on the wall arranged in order of size and were daring to stare at me! I strolled over and gazed up at them - and they looked down shyly at me. I felt a sudden pang of compassion as I looked at them, so young and innocent. At only a few months old they had their lives in front of them, and so who was I to act the grumpy old cat? So instead of giving them an earful, as had been my initial intention, I gave them my best Cheshire Cat grin and merely told them to be careful they didn't fall off the wall and to cling on tight to the bricks when they descended. I then nodded to them and returned to the kitchen via the dreaded cat flap.

7.30pm: I had been snoozing on my sofa following a somewhat unexceptional dinner when I heard the door into the motor machine's part of the house opening. Peter and Sheila's voices were pitched several tones higher than normal and they were obviously making encouraging noises to another cat - saying those soppy things humans say like "puss, puss, puss - here pussy, pussy", etc. I often wonder, what DO they think we are - as childish (kittenish, I mean!) as their own human babies? We cats are not stupid and don't need speaking to in kitten talk all our lives! Humans speak their 'baby' talk to their own little ones for several years - all that goo, goo, goo and gaa, gaa, gaa - what rubbish! Mother cats may well coo over their offspring initially, but in a couple of months we cats are comparatively grown up whilst baby humans take years and years. I do sometimes wonder why humans control the world - and not very well either! I'm sure feline power would make a great deal of difference and things would run much more smoothly! Anyway, I'm going off track again ...

I crept over behind them and could see that Chip was under one of the motor machines playing a game of hide and seek with them - much as my old friend, Pandy, used to do. The only way he could be persuaded to come out was by being given a tempting bit of food. Sensible lad, I thought - scrounging must run in the family! Once he had got his bit of food, Chip allowed Peter to pick him up and put him out into the garden. Peace reigned and we all moved into the lounge, where the humans ranged themselves in front of the silver box and prepared to transfix themselves on it for the rest of the evening. I sat on Sheila's knee, as usual, and started to think back again to past happenings.

8.30pm: I was in a reflective mood but had half an ear cocked as I was listening to some rather peculiar sounds that were emanating from the said silver box. Normally I can't make out what is happening in this magical box but occasionally some things catch my attention. The noises I seemed to be hearing at that moment sounded like birds chirping to me or perhaps various squeaks from small animals. There appeared to be an image on the screen of an elderly, somewhat short and portly human with a beard. This human was gesticulating wildly with his arms and brandishing some binoculars and was chattering non-stop about wildlife in general. The odd thing about it was that his name seemed to be Oddie! Peter and Sheila seemed glued to his comments. I watched for a few moments and thought I saw some rabbits jumping about - I shook my head - couldn't be - how could live rabbits get into the box? I must be hallucinating, I thought! Anyway, I turned around and curled up facing away from the box and remembered my own experience with a baby rabbit ...

It happened some years ago in the big garden. You will remember there was a large lake in the garden and running into it was a narrow, watery ditch with quite high grassy banks on each side bordered with rushes and other waterside plants. We cats used to like sitting there watching out for dragonflies and other tasty flying creatures that swarmed round the pond in the warm summer months. Anyway, one day Tansy, Lucky and I were sitting doing just that when we spotted a very tiny baby rabbit on the other side of the ditch stranded under a tree root with his paws stuck in the sticky mud. Cor, a sitting duck (no, a sitting rabbit!) we thought, so we immediately surrounded the little chap who - understandably - became somewhat agitated as he realised that he was going to end up as one of our dinners. Lucky had just managed to grab the rabbit by its neck when, by all the bad luck, Sheila came by and saw what was going on. She splashed some water at Lucky who fortunately managed to dodge it, but by that time he had lost his hold on the rabbit and so he ran off, us following. Sheila then became determined to rescue the rabbit. At that time her father was living in the house, so she called him to her aid and managed to clamber across the ditch to where the rabbit was trapped. Before she picked him up she put on some bright lurid pink rubber paw covers, which I should think nearly gave the rabbit a heart attack - I have only ever seen her wearing such things when doing the washing-up by hand (another silly task you humans seem to do - why, when a quick lick around with the tongue is surely enough?) The rabbit was so small that he fitted in completely beneath these pink monstrosities and Sheila carried him into the house. He was completely covered in yellowish-brown sticky mud and not a bit of fur was visible. Sheila and her father then proceeded to douse him in a basin of water - father held him down and Sheila washed him thoroughly with that peculiar little white brick you seem to use that turns into froth and foam. I was peeping round the corner whilst all this performance was going on, and after a few initial struggles the rabbit became butter in their paws. His coat also changed colour from the sludgy brown I described to a pale greyish white. I sighed - he looked more delectable now than he did when we had first spotted him in the ditch. Once clean, the rabbit was dried off with a towel and finally Sheila got out her fur-drying gadget and blow-dried his fur. Being so tiny, how the rabbit didn't have a heart attack I'll never know, but I guess he was so traumatised by the whole episode, he just went into a kind of trance and let her do whatever she wanted. I would, even myself, be a little wary of this strange hot air blowing machine, but as I just adore being warm, I think I could bear it!

Once Sheila was satisfied that the rabbit was all squeaky clean and furry, she put it into a box and awaited Peter's return home. I rather think she would have liked to keep the rabbit as a pet - and that would have been nice for we cats too - but Peter persuaded her not to do so and later on released the little rabbit back into the field beyond the pond where, presumably, it had ventured from in the first place. Lucky, I know, at first light went into the field to see if he could find it again, but was unsuccessful - the rabbit had gone to ground.

Who's a scaredy rabbit then?!

Left alone, we cats could very skilfully hunt and catch various small mammals, but the interference of our devoted human carers has saved many from our clutches over the years. Still, we were never hunting for food, as we've always been well cared for and looked after. It was just for the feline sport of things, so in the long run it never mattered to me that much whether I caught something or not. Lucky, on the other hand, was an experienced and skilful hunter, going back to his humble beginnings as a farmyard kitten where almost from day one he had to look after himself. Although he, too, had been well fed since being adopted by Sheila and Peter and had no real reason to kill, he never lost his urge to hunt.

11.00pm: We all rose from our positions in the lounge - the humans made their way upstairs and I headed for the kitchen and the haven of my bed. Another day over, another one to come ...

TUESDAY

6.30am: Unusually for me, I was awake early this morning - the bright rays of sunshine blasting through the newly installed window in my personal door alighted on my closed eyes and made me jump up with a start. Now fully awake, I found I actually wanted to go outside and make the most of this unusually fine weather. I could hardly wait to hear Peter's footstep outside the door. He, too, was taken aback to find me sitting at the door leading into the garden rather than curled in a tight ball in my comfy bed! I gave him a yowl to indicate that I wanted the door opening and he immediately obeyed my instruction without delay, so I sauntered out into the early morning sunshine, relishing its warmth on my backbone.

6.55am: Again, unusually for me, with no particular thoughts of breakfast on my mind I was lying on the patio having completed my daily ablutions in my private spot on the back flower bed. Mmm, the sun had really got a spurt on - even this early in the day - and all around me were the sounds of bees humming and the wings of those delectable little creatures you humans call butterflies were whirring into action. Taro, I remembered, was particularly fond of a butterfly as a snack and became quite an expert at catching them. Sheila was always berating him for this habit as she likes the little perishers. As for me, I find them rather irritating - all that flapping around making a disturbance as one tries to snooze in peace.

7.10am: Peter called out to tell me that my breakfast was ready, but I decided not to go in right away - a cat should never, but never, come immediately to a human's call. Stupid dogs, who are trained and are consequently under their humans' thumbs do just that, but to me it shows that they have no minds of their own and have to be told what to do all the time. Cats, on the other hand, definitely have minds of their own and will only respond to a human's call when and if it suits them. At the moment it certainly didn't suit me, so I ignored Peter and remained where I was. So pleasant ...

8.30am: Well, I must have dozed off again because now I did, indeed, feel rather hungry. I went into the kitchen - by this time Peter had departed - and inspected my bowl, which contained some quite tasty crunchies this morning plus some slivers of cold beef from the humans' dinner the previous evening. It all looked fairly acceptable so I soon disposed of this initial feast of the day. Yes, pretty yummy really, folks! I retired for a while to my bed to begin the whisker licking process that follows a meal and was in the middle of this task when Sheila came down. She greeted me in her usual affectionate manner and we spent a few moments idly chatting to each other. By this I mean that she says such silly, repetitive stuff like "Truffles, hello Truffles, good girlie, mummy's pet", etc. I chunter on in cat language which, of course, she doesn't understand, but I generally repeat the compliments. We actually adore each other, and since she stopped work about five or six years ago and became my main carer we have been constant companions. It seems a long time ago now when we were a family of five cats, plus the soppy, great dog and the large, evil, blue and yellow bird. All the other cats and dogs that Sheila and Peter looked after are now in various baskets in the cool blue heavens above, though the horrible bird, no doubt, is in a rather hotter neck of the woods down below! Now that I am nearing nineteen of your human years, I feel I am lucky to have outlived my peers and am now the sole recipient of my human carers' attentions. There's nothing like being spoilt is there? And I intend to make the most of it – there are several more years in this old pussy yet!

10.00am: Back on the patio again, I was lazily watching a group of flies as they wafted to and fro on the slight breeze that stirred the leaves of the spring flowers in the tubs around me. Suddenly there was a bump, and over the wall came Alfie from next door. Again, I have to admit he is a very handsome young tomcat with a winsome expression and I'm sure, had he the means, he would have made lots of conquests over the female cats in the neighbourhood. However, I understand that his owners had nipped all those thoughts of his in the bud, so now he could only look and not act. Oh well, I suppose it's one way of keeping the feline population down! I hear of so many unwanted young kittens who are unable to find decent human carers and end up being taken into animal prisons or worse. Alfie is - understandably - wary of me because I will not stand for any cheek or flirtation from youngsters such as he. As readers of my previous diaries will know, there was only one male I might have succumbed to and that was Lucky. However, as it was such a lovely day and I was also feeling in a sunny mood, I bestowed a Cheshire Cat smile on Alfie as he passed by and I reckon that made his day!

12.15pm: I awoke from my snoozing to the loud and somewhat frightening sound of a big, evil-smelling and noisy machine that was being walked up and down the grass lawn by Jason, the gardener, and there was another even more scary humming and whirring gadget being wielded by Mark, his colleague. These two humans look after the grass for Sheila and Peter. I just loathe these awful loud and smelly machines that are so threatening to we small, cat-sized persons, but I do have to admit that after they have been taken away the grass here is lovely and short and comfortable to lie on - no spiky bits and tufts to get your fur in a mess. I hurriedly crept out of the way and resited myself by the side of a pink-flowered shrub on the flower bed. After the vile machines had been switched off and sweet silence reigned again, the two men and Sheila gathered together on the patio, sipping that hot, frothy brown stuff that you humans like to drink. Jason, I noticed, also scoffed no less than four cream sponge cakes that Sheila had provided - how that man can eat; his poor wife, Sue, must be constantly cooking. Mark was more restrained - he only ate two! Every fortnight I notice they do their grass cutting in about ten minutes flat but spend about half an hour on their coffee break - something wrong there! Still, if this is what humans call work (the age-old subject I still just cannot understand as cats have no room for it in their lives), I guess it can't be as bad as they make out! Sometimes Sue accompanies them and they get the grass cut in nearly half the time, but even then the coffee break goes on for at least half an hour. Some humans have it with jam on, as they say!

12.45pm: The humans were still lolling about on the patio and I got to looking at them more closely. Jason, Sue and Sheila all have quite a lot of fur on their heads, but Mark has only got very, very short fur on his - in fact, you can hardly see it! I've noticed that male humans for some reason shave their heads and faces. Why? You would never get a cat shaving off its fur - fur is the most attractive part of a cat. So why do humans want to get rid of their fur? Going about in a skin with no fur covering would seem pretty gross to a cat, so I can't see why humans want to look that way. And think of the valuable eating and sleeping time they would save if they didn't shave! Oh well, cats will never understand humans and their strange whims. I turned over and went back to sleep - maybe by the time I woke up they'd be gone.

3.00pm: Well, I finally woke up and, yes, they had all gone. It was still lovely and warm, so I decided to remain in my comfy position for a while longer and got to pondering again about humans and their whims. When we all lived in the house with the big garden and lake, one day we noticed a strange black cat who appeared to have made a nest in one of the bushes. He seemed rather shy and each time one of us approached to try to make conversation he shrank back into hiding, but he stuck it out for several weeks, refusing to move and appearing determined to join our little group. Sheila had noticed him and put out food each evening, which he gratefully gobbled up. We were pretty certain he was homeless, but for what reason we had no idea. He didn't look particularly thin, but he was obviously very lonely. Eventually, Lucky and Tansy had a word with him and it seemed that his human carers had moved house and he had been abandoned. How awful. How could people do that? Never mind, we told him, you will be onto a good thing in this house as Sheila and Peter, our human carers, are a soft touch - they will take you in for sure! However, it turned out that we were wrong on this occasion, as we heard them talking about the situation at some length and it seemed that we five cats plus the dog and macaw were about all they could cope with. Then Sheila had an idea. She had an elderly human friend called Gwen who lived nearby - one of the few humans I never minded stroking me. As I think I've said in my previous diaries, normally I can't stand strange humans' sweaty, fat, sausage-like fingers messing up my fur. Gwen was another human who worshipped cats - she had had a beautiful, long-furred, black and white cat called Pepé for years and he was the most spoilt and pampered cat in existence I should think. He had Gwen completely under his paw and everything he wanted he got, and instantly! He had the best of food - no 'own brand' tins for him, but cooked fillets of chicken and salmon - and he was coiffed daily whereas we only had the fur dresser once a week. Not that we minded that though - I've never been all that keen on my tangles being tugged out! Anyway, some months previously Pepé had gone to that eternal cat basket in the sky and Gwen was bereft, so Sheila thought that she might like to adopt our little black waif. At first her pleas to Gwen fell on stony ground, as no cat would ever compare to the wonderful Pepé. However, Sheila artfully invited Gwen round at about the time that she usually fed the little black cat. Yes, dear reader, Gwen was immediately won over and she took the little cat back home with her that very day. I heard later that she had christened him Sam, and I believe that he remained her companion for several years after. We used to get quite a number of strange cats passing through our garden in those days, but no others ever tried to muscle in on our territory.

4.15pm: Dear me - with all this reminiscing I realised I had missed lunch! That would never do, so I got up and sauntered into the kitchen. Yes, there was some meat in the bowl ready for me, though, due to my own fault in appearing late, I noticed a pair of cheeky flies dining on it. I ate them as well - served them right, the dirty little beggars! I quite like the odd fly or spider or - even better - a daddy longlegs. You can have a lot of fun with them - patting them about and seeing how many of their legs fall off! Stupid creatures!

5.00pm: Back outside again and thinking of the odd creatures that we find in our gardens, I know that one of the ones that Sheila particularly loathes is that miraculous being called a slow-worm. They look like snakes but I believe they are actually legless lizards. I've heard of legless humans - when they have participated in too many of those sickly and fizzy drinks they seem to like – so perhaps lizards have the same addiction. Lucky told me once that, back in the old days, he was always being told off for catching slow-worms and bringing them back into the house. He thought it was a nice thing to do - to give Sheila a present as a thank you for all the things she did for him - but she felt otherwise. Very unappreciative, I thought. As I remember from my own experiences, a slow-worm can give a cat hours of pleasure. If you bite it into bits, each one wriggles independently and so you have several pieces to play with before deciding which bit to eat first. I used to like to eat the tail end first, but Lucky preferred the middle bit - he was rather a torturer - as he thought that the hapless slow-worm's head would still be able to see its tail but not its midriff! I have an idea that slow-worms are blind, but I never told Lucky this - it would have taken the shine off his little sadistic game! I remember, on one occasion, somehow three bits of slow-worm had slithered under the door of the cupboard beneath the stairs and come to rest under a box. When Sheila later opened the door, her scream could be heard round the entire village I reckon!

Let's have some fun!

8.00pm: After a light supper - I hadn't wanted very much since I'd had my lunch so late - we all sat outside in the garden as it was one of those rare, balmy, warm evenings that occasionally occur in spring here in Cornwall. For once the silver box was ignored and Peter snoozed in a garden chair whilst Sheila lolled in another and began clattering some plastic sticks in her hands to which was attached a long strand of wool. Wool - stuff we cats love! It smells of sheep but sheep are white and this wool was purple, so I couldn't get my head around that. Still, never mind, time for a little game! Even at my age, I still can't resist trying to catch at bits of wool. I repositioned myself by Sheila's side and stretched out a paw, hooking my claws into the strand of wool, which brought her clattering sticks to a halt. She then disentangled my claws only for me to repeat the performance! This happened no less than six times and I could see she was becoming rather irritated with me, so after a couple more tugs I finally decided to let her have her way and moved off, curling up on the patio to catch the last rays of the sunshine.

8.30pm: I was dozing with half an eye and ear open to catch the small sounds of creatures that were starting to emerge in the twilight. There were only small rodents around in this garden - in the big one we used to get a parade of foxes and their cubs and even, on occasions, a pair of badgers would trudge through. A well-worn path through our garden and into the one next door had been trodden by these nocturnal animals over the years. I never dared to approach any of them, preferring just to look from a distance. Lucky, needless to say, had chanced his luck once or twice, but even he had given up after being given short shrift by a rather spiteful vixen who was being overprotective of her two cubs and thought that Lucky presented a threat. A snarling fox and its offspring scared even him!

10.15pm: Tonight I turned in early. Once we had come in from outdoors it suddenly seemed to turn chilly, so my furry bed looked overly tempting. Pausing only to use the services of my cat litter igloo, I crawled into my bed, had a nice scratch and settled down for the rest of the night. Sweet dreams beckoned ...

WEDNESDAY

6.45am: Well, yesterday's early rising was a one-off! If Peter expected me to be up and bouncing around two days running he was going to be unlucky! Despite his entreaties for me to get up and go outside, I studiously ignored him and curled up in my bed, determined to have a bit more sleep time. I could hear him going about his duties - cleaning the litter from the igloo and emptying the dregs from my bowl before refilling it with today's breakfast. I would examine that in a moment - meanwhile I dozed off again whilst he ate his own breakfast of that dry-looking crunchy stuff you humans like to eat, though I am pleased to note that at least you do add milk to it. None of you seems to drink enough of the white stuff - no wonder you don't have long fur and shiny eyes! A lifelong obsession with this delicious liquid has kept me in good working order. Good meaty meals with the odd delicacy of bird or mouse - complete with their crunchy bones for my teeth - have also helped me keep in the good health I am still enjoying today. I can swear, paw on heart, that to date I have never had to have any treatment from the vet, unlike several of my past feline and canine pals.

7.45am: I woke up, had a stretch and made my way over to the bowl, sniffing to see what delights were in store for me - something fishy, not sure exactly what, but it wasn't too bad. I then performed my ablutions in the igloo litter box and went out into the garden to see what was happening. No sooner had I arrived on the patio than I heard a cacophony of squeaking and yapping from the two little whippersnappers of dogs that live next door. One, as I told you in the catch-up at the beginning of this diary, is an absolute hooligan of a West Highland terrier called Oscar and the other is a spoilt little brat of a shih-tzu called Princess. They appeared to be having a real argy-bargy. What a racket! I cannot understand why dogs have to be so very noisy - apart from the odd occasion when a group of felines get together for an argument, cats are generally so very quiet and well behaved. Dogs, on the other hand, are one of the loudest and most uncouth animals one could meet in my opinion. In saying this, I have to admit that Hennessy the St Bernard was not a noisy dog at all - he never barked if anyone came to the door, but when he DID decide to bark, well, it was like a roll of thunder! You had to cover your ears with your paws - it was like World War III was approaching! It was certainly better, though, than the incessant yapping that was coming from next door. I peered through a crack in the wall and could see the two little dogs circling around a ginger cat that had mistakenly decided to do a spot of sunbathing in their garden. Living with six cats of their own, Oscar and Princess didn't usually make a lot of fuss, but any strange cat was in for a basinful of abuse if it dared to enter their domain! The small ginger cat was called Harry and I had seen him around here before - don't know where he lives exactly but it can't be far away. Rather like Lucky - my hero - he was a plucky little fellow and stood his ground. Of course he knew that if it came to a chase, well, the stupid dogs would have no chance as he could run rings round them! For the moment, though, he was brave enough to stay put even though their shrill yapping must have made his eardrums rattle. I watched and waited ...

8.00am: Suddenly Harry decided to make a move, and as he lightly sprang to his paws, intending to move to a more sheltered spot to continue his sunbathing in peace, both little dogs immediately jumped at him in hot pursuit. Harry deftly avoided them by leaping up onto a steep grassy bank but Oscar, with Princess hot on his heels, also attempted to negotiate the bank in an effort to grab Harry. Unfortunately this was his downfall because, lunging at Harry, he managed to catch his collar on a stout twig and nearly strangled himself - he was left hanging in space suspended by his tartan collar. His ferocious yapping turned into squeals of panic - I had to smile! Served the little bounder right - never attempt to harass a cat, as it's a no-win situation! I was surprised that the neighbours hadn't heard all the noise and come out to see what was happening, but their back door remained closed. Maybe they had gone out somewhere ...

8.15am: The scenario was much the same - Oscar hanging by his collar with Harry above him, quietly smirking, and Princess running hither and thither below. I was rather enjoying myself. It was nice to see two bolshy little dogs cut down to size! Oscar was wriggling like mad and snivelling as he waited to be rescued. A cat by now would have thought up a plan of escape and would have somehow managed to cling on to the offending twig with its claws and unhook the collar - but, of course, I forget, dogs have no intelligence and would never think of doing that, so he was well and truly stuck! Princess was no help, as by now she had wandered away. She was probably thinking about her next visit to the fur dresser - I know that she is regularly taken to the professionals who crimp and curl her fur and bathe her, etc. What a sissy! At least she doesn't have ribbons in her hair, but I believe she actually has various outer coverings like you humans do - coats and scarves, etc.

9.30am: I heard next door's humans come out into the garden. Yes, I had been right, they had indeed been out somewhere and had left the dogs out in the garden - safe as they had thought! Screams of horror at seeing Oscar suspended above the bank rang out, and Harry fled. Oscar was now something of a quivering jelly and was all too eager to be picked up in strong arms. As Harry had disappeared from view, the humans had no idea as to how or why Oscar had become entangled on the twig, and instead of being comforted, as he had anticipated, he was shouted at for being a naughty boy and grilled as to why on earth he had been trying to get up the bank. Oscar was often in trouble for getting out of the garden and escaping and his human carers were for ever reinforcing the fencing and the grassy bank around their garden. So today he was in trouble again for, as they thought, trying to escape! Well, as I've said before, dogs should never try to tangle with a cat - they always come off worst. Harry had won the day and, as Oscar was then grounded indoors for the rest of it, he could enjoy his sunbathing in peace!

What a soppy dog - not so bold and bolshy now!

10.30am: I wandered indoors and settled down on my rug in front of the patio doors - a nice suntrap when we get any. So far today the sun had not decided to put his hat on, but I held out hopes that he would do so shortly. My mid-morning sleep beckoned.

1.30pm: I awoke to find the sun streaming in onto my back and my fur was nice and warm. I stretched luxuriously and went into the kitchen where I could hear Sheila clattering about with some pots and pans. I indicated to her that I wanted my lunch so, being the well-trained carer that she is, she stopped what she was doing and filled my bowl with some quite delicious morsels of prawns and haddock. I must say that my training over the years has made her into an obedient servant who knows my exacting requirements as set out in her personal job description. I do appreciate this, even though on occasions I have had to reprimand her when she's tried to fob me off with supermarket 'own brand' cat foods or inferior brands. It's my insistence on being properly looked after that has given me this longevity of life and I intend to keep things this way for as long as I can!

3.00pm: I settled back down in my sunny spot on the rug again. The sun was now definitely doing his best and, as I thought about that silly dog, Oscar, dangling by his collar, I remembered a similar funny event that happened years ago with the basset hound, Lady. I never knew Lady myself, but Lucky had told me about her and the stupid things she got up to. As every cat knows, of all dogs bassets are one of the dimmest breeds. Lady certainly lived up to that reputation, as readers of my previous diaries will have seen! Anyway, Sheila was out with Lady, taking her for a long ramble over some fields near to where they used to live. All was going well and the pair of them were contentedly ambling along, Lady snuffling around in the grass as usual and Sheila daydreaming as she strolled slowly, enjoying the peacefulness of the countryside. They were skirting a field that contained some of those rather smelly creatures called cows - yet more of nature's dimmest! There used to be several young cows that lived in a field adjacent to our previous house and sometimes I used to sit and watch them. What an odd bunch - they just ambled about all day chewing and chewing and emitting revolting smells and noises from their mucky-looking rear ends. Disgusting behaviour - something cats would never do! One thing we do carry out to extremes in the cat world is keeping our bottoms clean - in fact, there is a well-known cat saying, 'When in doubt, sit down and lick backside'. A consequence of this, of course, is that we have immaculate bottoms! However, to get off this rather unsavoury subject, I will continue with my tale about Sheila and Lady's experience with the cows ... There were about ten or so of them in the field, huddled together in a group in the far corner - nowhere near Lady and Sheila. They looked pretty peaceful and Sheila intended to continue walking around the field without disturbing them. Lady, however, oblivious to Sheila's 'keep our distance' strategy, found a particularly interesting smell and all of a sudden upped her speed and started to trot quite swiftly in the direction of the cows. Despite Sheila calling her, Lady continued on this perilous route and, needless to say, the cows saw her, raised their heads in unison from the grass they were chewing and, with a number of grunts and bellows, with one accord they started moving towards Lady in quite an aggressive manner! The lead cow then lowered its head and quickened its pace. The rest followed. Lady, suddenly realising that these animals were somewhat larger than she was and that they also appeared extremely irritated, turned tail and ran towards Sheila who immediately clipped on her lead and attempted to walk smartly back in the direction they had come from without actually panicking and running - she hoped the cows would turn away and leave them to it. However, the cows put on a turn of speed and were now approaching at a frightening pace, so Sheila began to run, hauling Lady along behind her. They came to the edge of the field with the cows in hot pursuit, only to realise that the gate was still several metres away and that quite a deep ditch confronted them before they could escape into the lane. With the cows virtually breathing down her neck, Sheila scrambled over the ditch, pulling Lady with her. However, as Lady's legs were so short, she couldn't jump the ditch and only by Sheila hanging on to her collar was she saved from the marauding cows - she was suspended over the ditch with her back legs trailing in the mud. Fortunately her heavy collar held, and once she had scrambled over the other side Sheila managed to haul Lady up by the said collar. It was a narrow squeak for the pair of them! The cows, fortunately, came to a halt at the ditch and Sheila and Lady flopped down exhausted on the other side, but safe! With a few trumpeting moos, the cows returned to their peaceful selves and their grazing. Sheila and Lady stayed where they were for a while to catch their breath and then legged it home as fast as they could!

6.oopm: Supper time once more - an incentive to move myself! I wandered into the kitchen - something smelled good. Sheila was removing a container from the mysterious little box that lives on the worktop in which she puts one thing and out comes something else - like a magician pulling a rabbit out of a hat! I really do not understand it at all. She usually puts in cardboard boxes of cold, uninteresting-smelling stuff that, amazingly, come out a few minutes later steaming and smelling delicious! Some other nice things she puts in are what you humans call Cornish pasties - I don't think Sheila makes these herself, but once in this little box they soon get hot and smell and taste absolutely wonderful. I am usually given a piece of pasty when they have them and I love it. Tonight's offering didn't smell of pasty, however, but more like something oriental, and as I am not so fond of that particular flavouring I contented myself with what was in my own bowl - some nice cod pieces, as it happened, in a savoury sauce.

6.15pm: Well, yummy - I really enjoyed the cod. Cleaned the bowl out. Talking of clean bowls, as I have said before, I cannot understand why you humans have so many bowls to eat your food from. Why? So unnecessary! Sheila always complains about the washing-up and also how Peter never helps her with it, but if they were sensible they would realise that you only need one bowl for food and one for water like we cats do and - bingo! - no moans, no wasted time scouring pots and pans and dishes, and much longer sleeping time. Well, I scratch my head over your strange habits - really I do! Talking of scratching, there's nothing like a good, long, leisurely scratch, so I decided to have one. Lovely! Once I started, I really didn't want to stop, so I must have kept it up for about five minutes or so. You get into a rhythm and just want to go on and on and on - a very satisfying feeling. I must assure you right away, though, that I scratch for pure pleasure only - I do not have any of those nasty little creatures called fleas or ticks on me. Sheila gives me a treatment probably every couple of months or so that keeps them well at bay.

8.30pm: By this time we were ensconced in the lounge as usual in front of the silver box, with Peter slumped in his chair making those revolting roaring and whistling noises that human males seem to make when their eyes are closed. Sheila was busy doing one of her puzzles - crosswords she calls them. Now that's a funny thing to call them - why 'cross' words and not 'happy' words? It seems to keep her happy doing these puzzles, so why should she call them cross? Another anomaly about the human language that I can't get my head around!

9.15pm: I had been quite comfortably positioned on Sheila's knee for some time, but now she was beginning to annoy me by shifting position from time to time, nearly knocking me onto the floor at one point. She seemed to be complaining about how stiff and sore her hips were. I must say I have noticed lately she has been hobbling very slowly around the house and has been having to use two sticks to help her. I think I've heard her say to friends that she's waiting for two new hip joints. Well, I'm sorry to hear she needs new hips - I wonder why? I have four of my own and they are absolutely fine and, in terms of age, in human years I am much older than she is. There you go, proof again that a cat's lifestyle is more healthy than a human's!

9.30pm: I remember once that Geronimo, the foul-mouthed blue and gold macaw, had some problem with one of his legs and for a time it was encased in a surgical boot so that he couldn't move about very much. During that time - I guess it must have been about two or three weeks - he shouted and swore at us all even more than usual! It was quite terrifying for small pussy persons like us to be subjected to such language. I don't know where he learned the words from - Peter I suppose taught him some of them, certainly not Sheila! Geronimo would imitate what he heard the humans say - he hadn't the brain to speak just off his own bat. All he could do was repeat odd words or phrases that took his fancy, but the humans who heard him thought he was very clever. He knew all our names, so out of the blue he would sometimes call out "Puss, puss, puss - come on Truffles, come on Truffles", having listened to Sheila or Peter calling me at some point. Many's the time I've been woken up on hearing my name being called and expected that a meal was ready and then found out it was just that pesky macaw. Wretched bird! I understand the human language very well, but then, of course, as you know, I am a particularly clever feline. However, I don't speak it or attempt to. Much better to let the humans think I don't understand what they say half the time - it gives me a huge advantage! Of course, none of them can understand cat language, so I can say what I like to them - insults or whatever - and they just smile and say something like, "Oh, she's answering you back. How sweet"!

10.15pm: Peter had already gone up to his bed and Sheila decided to have an early night too to rest her troublesome hips, so she woke me up from my dozing and folded up her puzzle paper and we walked slowly into the kitchen together where she patted me, kissed me goodnight and saw me into bed. Ah - it's so nice to feel loved! And as for an early night with an extra hour or so of proper sleep – well, I'm not one to say no to that, am I?

THURSDAY

7.00am: Well, another day has dawned, a nice one, too. I strolled to the cat flap and peered out - yes, Mr Sun's hat was well and truly on his head and his rays were simply pouring out, aiming right in my direction. I could feel the warmth even at this ungodly hour in the morning. I felt optimistic that this might well be the hottest day of the year so far and I looked forward to a pleasant day lazing in the garden. Peter was already at work on the litter igloo and my breakfast was in its bowl, so I ate the pâté of sardine and prawn quite quickly. It was nice - not outstanding, but in the expectant mood I was in, I felt I must get outside as soon as possible.

7.20am: My morning ablutions having been carried out on the back flower bed, I settled down by the back doorstep and comfortably arranged myself at just the right angle to catch the warming rays on my back - ah, a lovely feeling! My eyes were closing already. However, a flash of ginger amongst the bushes caught my attention, so I raised myself up and saw that Harry, the young ginger cat who lived somewhere nearby, was sitting looking at me. He has been around for a couple of months now and Sheila first noticed him when he was really quite small and was struggling to climb the wall into the next door garden. She called him and picked him up, thus discovering his name, which was on the blue collar he was wearing, and put him on the spot he was trying to reach. Since then he has visited regularly on his way to play with the other kittens next door. I, of course, am too senior a cat to 'play' with kittens. Although, as you know, I do not like other cats invading my territory, there is something about young Harry - his innocence and friendliness perhaps - that makes me more tolerant of him than the others. Everyone seems to like Harry - humans and other cats alike. He seems to be in next door's garden most days and even the two hooligan dogs do not phase him, as I told you before.

7.30am: Harry tentatively approached me and I waved a paw, indicating that he could sit beside me for a while and enjoy the sunshine too. It was perhaps a little too early for him to start playing with the others - I hadn't heard their cat flap opening yet anyway. Harry lay down beside me and shyly asked how I was. Quite well, I assured him, and we spent the next hour or so companionably enjoying the sunshine.

9.15am: Harry was about to go next door to see if anyone was out and I gather he also intended to climb one of the trees to do a bit of bird stalking. Before he went, I told him about an incident involving Tansy and a tree that had happened when we all lived in our lovely big garden a few years ago. To be honest, Tansy and trees never got on too well and usually there was water in the scenario as well and she was for ever unlucky in that respect. Readers of my previous diary will probably remember the time that she got stranded on the island in the middle of the lake!

9.25am: All ears, Harry settled down again to hear about Tansy's adventure. It happened when Tansy and I were quite small and hadn't been with Sheila and Peter in our new home all that long. We were totally gobsmacked at the size of the garden and the huge expanse of water, which fascinated us both as we used to love watching all the little aquatic creatures that lived in and around it on its grassy banks. Tansy, in particular, liked to watch the silver, red and gold flashes of the fish that lived in the lake and spent hours perched on the stone-edged steps that led down to the water, hoping to hook one in. She never had any luck! She also liked to try to catch small frogs that hopped occasionally onto the bank and the damsel and dragonflies that hovered above, glistening in the sun. All in all there is something magnetic about water to we cats. Though we loathe getting ourselves wet and being IN the water, we love the ambience and the sparkle of it. Around the pond grew various water plants and reeds, including some absolutely enormous plants with giant leaves, each about one metre or more wide - I kid you not - Sheila has some photos of me and Tansy sitting on these huge leaves. They were pretty prickly as I remember and the whole plant had a rather rude-sounding name in your human language, but is often known as Chilean Rhubarb for some reason. One day I was lying on the bank and Tansy was daydreaming and looking into the water as usual, when she spotted a couple of quite large fish idling nearby. To get a better view, she climbed up onto the lower branches of an overhanging willow tree. Unfortunately for her, the thin branch bent under even her slight weight and she was catapulted onto one of the huge prickly leaves of the Chilean Rhubarb - which, in turn, acted as a springboard and bounced her up onto another leaf at a higher level! Honestly, you couldn't have done that if you'd tried! Anyway, this second leaf then flopped downwards and Tansy was put into a very precarious position, clinging on for grim death with her front claws, high up above the very cold-looking water below! Her sharp claws gradually tore through the leaf and she could feel herself slowly slipping down it with the awful realisation that she was very shortly going to be plunged into the depths of the pond! She shrieked for help and Sheila came rushing up, followed by Hennessy the St Bernard dog. Sheila just hopped from side to side and was no help at all, and Hennessy lolloped around equally unhelpfully. What a to-do! Then Peter appeared and all he could do was laugh and say something about how this would be good on - well, I think he said something like 'Are You Being Framed' – but it didn't make sense to me. Myself, Hennessy and the humans were watching, all of us smiling to ourselves as it really was rather funny - but Tansy didn't see it that way at all! She began panicking and scrabbling at the leaf, which by now was getting somewhat ripped by her claws and, even though it was so thick and leathery and should ordinarily have supported her, we could almost see in slow motion that she was going to fall in - and fall in she soon did, splash! Neither Sheila nor Peter could have reached the leaf without falling in themselves, so it was inevitable that the whole episode was going to end in disaster for Tansy! Luckily she tumbled into the edge of the pond where the water wasn't so deep and managed to scramble ashore with her fur in great disarray, her pride fallen and her temper lost, but she WAS safe! Sheila scooped her up and rushed indoors and she was dried off (like the baby rabbit!) and though she sulked for the rest of the day (Tansy, I mean, not Sheila) we other cats chuckled amongst ourselves and told her she should look before she leaps in future! So I told Harry that he should also remember the old adage when he was climbing trees - look before you leap! Off he went, much the wiser, and I curled up and went into sleep mode again ...

Tansy's slide to disaster!

11.45am: I woke up smelling the scent of that brown frothy stuff that Sheila likes to drink. She was sitting on the wooden seat with a mug of it beside her and a pile of those celebrity magazines she likes to read. I am afraid she will never be a celebrity - not like me. I am definitely a celebrity after letting the human public see my private diaries and, as cats are not known for their modesty, I don't mind saying that if you have it, well flaunt it! When we get visitors they always seem amazed that I am (a) coming up to nineteen in human years, and (b) able to write! So I preen myself, but I don't usually go so far as to let them pat me unless they are very intimate acquaintances. After all, you don't let someone touch you if you don't know where they've been and whether their paws are clean. Well, that's my excuse and I am sticking to it!

1.00pm: Sheila went indoors, saying something about having a quick shower before lunch as it was so hot. Showering - another strange human habit and a complete and utter waste of water and time. We cats have regular quick licks all over, reaching right into all our intimate little places so we stay absolutely pristine and cool in the hot weather. I suppose, though, when you come to think of it, you humans are not designed to bend over and lick your own little intimate places, so I guess a shower has to be the next best thing!

2.30pm: I had eaten my lunch, which was nothing out of the ordinary, I'm afraid - I don't think Sheila makes the effort when it's hot - and I was curled up ready for my afternoon sleep session. I remembered how Taro, the Birman aristocat who used to live with us, did have some very out of the ordinary lunches! Again, when we lived in the other house, he used to disappear regularly on Mondays, Wednesdays and Fridays always at noon, come what may, whatever the weather. Sheila could hear him meowing but could never see exactly where he was - she knew he wasn't that far away, but she was never able to see him even though she did try several times. It was very odd. This went on for about six months or more and then one day suddenly Taro stopped going out and disappearing at that time. Stranger and stranger! A little while later the mystery was solved, however. Several smaller gardens bordered onto our large one, each one belonging to a small one-storey building I believe you humans call a bingo, or bongo, or bungo, or something similar - anyway, somewhere where elderly humans who've stopped doing that odd thing called work live. Apparently one elderly male human used to have what you call 'Meals on Wheels' three days a week delivered to him. He could never eat all of it and so Taro, who happened to be passing one day, was offered a plateful by the old man. This became a habit and Sheila heard from the old man's neighbour that every day, just before the expected meal-delivery time, there was Taro sitting on the man's dustbin, calling to tell him that he was ready for his food! Sadly the old man went to that home that humans go to in the sky and, from that very day on, Taro never went there again. Somehow he must have known that the old man had gone - Sheila had no idea, so it must have been a case of a cat's extrasensory perception. I'm sure you all know that some cats have something of a second sight and can often foretell things to come or other odd phenomena. I have to say that, despite all my other attributes, I do not have this power myself, but Taro, being of oriental origin, may have inherited this power from his centuries-old ancestors.

Taro enjoying his "Meals on Wheels"

4.00pm: The sun was still shining brightly and had moved across the garden, so I changed my position to feel its warming rays on my fur. No matter how hot or cold the weather is, I can never get enough heat on my fur! Sometimes I watch Sheila when she washes her own fur that grows on her head and she uses the little machine that she blow-dried the rabbit with. It gives out a lovely, soothing heat. However, she has never offered me the chance to use it. Although generally I loathe and am frightened of the various bits of equipment she uses (yes, I admit it, your human noisy machines scare a little pussy-sized person like me to death!), I am not frightened of this particular one. I think it must be lovely and soothing to have a hot blow-dry on your fur - but to date I have never had one. I suppose if I stayed out when those drops of water fall out of the sky and got drenched, she might give it a go, but I'm afraid there's no way I could stay out and get all wet - just alien to a cat's nature! Oh well, I guess I'll never experience a blow dry ...

4.10pm: I was nicely settled and sleep was about to overcome me again when I remembered a cat joke that you may like to hear. It was recalling Taro's meals with the old human that reminded me! Here we go then ... There once was a nice little cat who sadly died and went to that place you humans call 'heaven'. After he had been there a week or so, God (who apparently is the owner of heaven) came along to see how he was settling in. "Hello cat," he said, "how are you doing?" "Well," replied the cat, "it seems very nice here and I think I will like it." God looked at the clipboard he was carrying with the cat's details on it and said that he had heard the cat had been a very good little cat whilst on Earth, so he would like to reward him with a gift. So he asked the cat what he would like. The cat said that he had always wanted one of those squashy, comfy beanbag beds, but his owners had not given him one. "Well, that's okay," said God, "I will get one for you," and on his way he went. Shortly after, God came across three little mice who had also just entered heaven. They, too, were busy settling into their new quarters. "Hello," said God, "I hear you were very good little mice when you were living on Earth, so you are due a gift as a reward. What would you like?" "Well, sir," replied one of the mice, "we run fast but we've always wanted roller skates so we can go even faster. Would that be possible?" "Of course," smiled God, "I will arrange it." A month or so went by and God, again, was doing his rounds. He came across the cat again, who was lying in the sun, sprawled out on his comfy beanbag bed, looking happy and content. "Oh," said God, "you're enjoying life up here then?" "Oh yes," replied the cat, "I just love it - the sun is shining all the time, my bed is so comfortable and the meals on wheels are just superb"!

6.00pm: My tummy was rumbling, so I made my way to the kitchen. I could smell something nice, though I couldn't quite put my paw on what exactly it was. I could see that Sheila was looking busy again, standing by that marvellous, magical, oblong box. I wondered what delights were going to appear from it tonight. I must say I've never been disappointed yet. I've heard Peter say - somewhat disparagingly I reckon - that Sheila couldn't live without this box and he certainly wouldn't get any decent meals if she didn't have it! I give up trying to understand your human technology and I, for once, DO admit that we felines lag far behind in this field. Still, to be honest, simple mice, birds or cold cuts of meat or fish are all that we cats require to keep us fit and healthy and therefore there is no need for wasting hours (or, in Sheila's case - with the use of her little oblong box - minutes) of preparation time when you could be using the time in more gainful ways, like sleeping! Anyway, whatever she was bringing out of the box really smelled nice. I wormed my way around her legs and she looked down and laughed – "Well, Truffles," she said, "I don't think you'll like this but you can try it if you like." I was immediately suspicious - I could tell she was teasing me! She picked up my dish and put a bit of the stuff in it. I approached it cautiously. Well, it certainly looked good - why wouldn't I like it? I took a tentative bite - cor blimey! - and leapt back. It was hot, hot, HOT! And, to a cat, totally revolting! Sheila burst out laughing - the rotter! "That'll teach you to go begging," she told me. "That's something called a vegetable chilli. You won't do that again!" "No, I certainly won't," I muttered to myself as I ran towards the water bowl.

8.15pm: After the chilli fiasco, I ate a nice, 'ordinary' sardine pâté supper and we all sat down again in the lounge in front of the infernal silver box for the evening. My 'feathers', which had been thoroughly 'ruffled' during the drama in the kitchen, calmed down and I prepared for another dozing and reminiscing session whilst they gazed, entranced, at the mysterious pictures coming and going on the silver box.

8.30pm: I looked back at the happy times I had with my old friends, particularly Tansy and Lucky, at our old house. I think I already told readers in my previous books that Lucky was found by Sheila and Peter when he was a young kitten, lying injured in the road. He had apparently come from a farm and nobody seemed to want him; nobody wanted to help him either. So after a visit to the vet, who patched him up, Lucky moved in with Sheila and Peter. By the time I came on the scene and first met him, he was about four or five years old. I liked him immediately. Although some of my more well-bred feline acquaintances might have described Lucky as 'a bit of rough', I could see that underneath the somewhat unpolished exterior he had a heart of gold and was also very feisty and self-sufficient - something I admire in a male cat. He was a ginger boy, pale in colour, with a white front and paws. He was the only one of the feline family that I could really talk to about stuff. Tansy, of course, was my other confidante, but she was a bit of an airhead. Lucky always had an interesting story to tell and could remember many things that had happened in his life on the farm before he joined our happy band. One thing that made me smile was when he told me about the mole. Apparently there were a lot of moles living in the fields and the farmer was always cross when yet another new molehill appeared overnight in his strawberry patch. Part of his livelihood was to allow other humans to come along to pick and purchase his strawberries so he liked the field to look smart, and the strawberry beds criss-crossed with smooth paths so that humans could walk on them without getting their paws all muddy. Paths strewn with molehills was not what he wished to see!

Lucky and the other cats and kittens who lived in the farmyard liked to see if they could catch the culprit moles - not because of their molehills but because apparently moles taste quite nice (not that I have ever had the pleasure of eating one myself). On this particular morning, very early, Lucky was prowling around the strawberry patch and came across a large mole sitting all alone, surveying his latest edifice. Immediately Lucky pounced and - joy, oh joy - got a large mouthful of mole's back leg. He hung on tight, intending to try to whip the mole around and snap its neck (sorry if you are a bit squeamish, dear reader!) However, understandably, the mole had other ideas. As I said, it was quite large and Lucky was still very young, so there was really not much difference in size. Lucky was also very inexperienced then as a hunter - not the professional he was when I met him.

Anyway, the mole took off with Lucky hanging on behind him for dear life. For a few feet Lucky was dragged along and then suddenly he was plunged into darkness as the mole hurtled head first into his burrow. The tunnel immediately became narrower and the mole dug wildly with its strong front claws, going deeper and deeper. He was slimmer than Lucky and consequently Lucky became wedged in the tunnel and was forced to relinquish his grip on the mole. How frustrating that must have been for Lucky - so near and yet so far! Of course, Lucky was now totally stuck and couldn't turn around to get out. The mole had disappeared way into the depths, so what was he to do? Lucky wriggled and wriggled and struggled and struggled, but it was no good - he just couldn't turn around to face the entrance of the burrow. As he was so young, he started crying - something he would never have dreamt of doing when he was fully grown and had become a real macho cat. Fortunately some human on the farm heard him and came to investigate. All this guy could see was the tip of a ginger and white tail hanging out of a hole in the strawberry patch, wagging wildly! Lucky was pulled ignominiously out of the hole by his tail and then berated by the human because after all the fuss he hadn't actually caught the mole. So, all in all, a disappointing result for all - except the mole! Perhaps that's why when Lucky was found after his road accident, the people on the farm didn't care enough about him to want to help him. How cruel some humans can be. Oh well, another reason why Lucky was always so independent - he was used to fending for himself. He truly did love living with Sheila and Peter and being looked after and given lots of TLC, but if for some reason he had been evicted he, out of us all, would have coped well with living and looking after himself in the wild, as he knew all the tricks needed to find food and shelter.

10.40pm: Well, it was time for bed, so we all vacated the lounge, the silver box went dark, and that was another day gone by. As I settled down for the rest of the night, I looked forward to some more sweet dreams ...

FRIDAY

7.10am: The unexpected good weather was continuing. Mr Sun's brilliant rays were penetrating the cat flap and catching me full in the face. I awoke with a start. Peter was not yet down - must have overslept. I had a nice stretch and dealt with an itchy ear before strolling to look out into the garden. Yes, it looked lovely and I - unusually for me, I know - felt an immediate desire to be up and about and all thoughts of further sleep fell quickly away. But, I thought, typical - on the odd occasion when I actually WANT to go out, there is no human at hand to unlock the door! This situation would not do at all, so I went to the inner kitchen door that leads into the hall and set up an immediate caterwaul to remind Peter or Sheila (well, not her I guess, because she would never arrive downstairs at such an early hour in the morning!) that they needed to appear down here pretty pronto. I kept up my calling, increasing the volume, for about five minutes until at last Peter put in an appearance. He seemed rather flustered and was a bit curt with me, telling me to "shut up" - how very rude, I thought - nobody tells ME to shut up! Ears flat, I circled him and made my feelings pretty evident. He was muttering that he had overslept and would be late for work, but would still have to deal with sorting the cat out for the morning, which was a pain. That made me even more cross - what? Me - a pain? Never! Anyway, whilst I watched, he stamped around in a foul mood, but he did clean the litter in a perfunctory sort of way, slapped my bowl down and unlocked the cat flap. Then he was off. Good job too, I thought. I was really feeling irritable now - my initial plan of waking up to what I had anticipated was going to be a perfect day had gone well and truly down the plughole. Woe betide anyone who crossed me now! I had no particular taste for my breakfast, so I just nibbled at it, performed in the litter igloo and made my way out of the cat flap.

7.30am: I sat on the patio sulking.

8.30am: Still sulking.

9.20am: I heard movement and Sheila stepped onto the patio behind me. I didn't acknowledge her. "Whatever's up, Truffles?" she asked. "Why's your tail wagging so?" I was just about to turn round but then suddenly she burst into that idiotic sound that you humans make - laughter, I think it is. Certainly we cats do not make such a ridiculous noise, nor any other animals I know of except perhaps the aptly named laughing hyena or kookaburra. I looked up quickly at her, but she was leaning over the fence and she and the neighbouring human who was standing on the other side were both howling with this dreadful sound of laughter. It went on and on and I began to fear for their sanity. Curiosity, of course, got the better of me, and so, my sulks forgotten, I went over and peered through a crack in the fence. All I could see was that stupid little shih-tzu, Princess, careering around the garden dragging a seemingly never-ending narrow strip of white paper, which appeared to have somehow got caught on one of her teeth and then somehow entwined itself with the buckle on her collar. Faster and faster she galloped around, leaving the paper festooned all around the plants and bushes until at last the paper trail finally came to a stop. The garden looked a complete shambles. Sheila and the neighbour, Jo, were still in a collapsed, hysterical state and Princess was by now cowering on the ground completely exhausted. What a to-do, I thought, and typical of a stupid dog - no cat would have allowed itself to become so entangled in anything. After a while, Sheila and Jo stopped their ghastly laughing and Jo began to clear up the offending strip of paper, which looked about a mile long to me. Whatever was it, I wondered, and where had it come from? My question was soon answered - though I was not exactly sure what they meant - when the other neighbour, Mandy, appeared and told Jo and Sheila that Princess must have been upstairs in the area where humans carry out their ablutions and, for some unaccountable reason, had grabbed this strip of paper from a roll and presumably run off with it stuck on her tooth. The three humans started their ghastly laughing yet again and kept on mentioning something about baby Labrador puppies and advertising. I was now thoroughly confused - the phrase 'barking' in respect of all of them sprang to mind, so I retreated again to my spot on the patio, which was now nicely warmed up by the sun.

10.30am: Peace and normality had once more returned and I was enjoying my mid-morning snooze, just pleased to be in the warm sun and listening to the odd rustle of leaves in the light breeze, the only interruption being the clink of cup on saucer as Sheila sat nearby sipping her regular hot brown frothy drink. Occasionally she gave a groan and I realised that her hips were aching. Today she was hobbling around really slowly on her two sticks and, I thought, didn't look all that happy. I hoped she could arrange to see her vet soon so that her hips could be put right. She had been taking rather a long time lately to see to my requirements and I didn't want this state of affairs to continue any longer than it had to. I resolved to see if I could cheer her up, so I went over and nuzzled around her legs. She picked me up, sat me on her lap and began patting me - it was a nice, almost hypnotic feeling and my eyes slowly closed. We sat peacefully together for the next hour or two.

1.15pm: Lunchtime. Sheila made her slow way into the kitchen and laboriously reached down for my bowl. Today she seemed to take ages filling it and replacing it, by which time my good mood had evaporated somewhat. I was feeling rather peckish by now. I was about to give her a loud meow to remind her to hurry up, but then I thought better of it - she was obviously having a bad day and even I must be tolerant on occasions. Normally I expect my carers to cater for my every whim immediately, but there must be a bit of give and take in our lives so that we all live together amicably - this was such an occasion. So I kept quiet. Anyway, when the bowl finally did arrive duly filled, it was a delicious mix of prawns and salmon topped with some kind of anchovy dressing. Mmm - delectable. My good humour returned as I cleaned out the bowl.

2.00pm: I was now comfortably ensconced on my mat inside the patio door and was in reminiscing mood once more. I suddenly began thinking about Robbie, another ginger and white cat, who only had one eye and lived with us all in the previous house. Unlike Lucky, who was a loner and a survivor, Robbie was very humanised as he had spent the first part of his life, probably about ten years, living with an elderly human all alone, enclosed in a small townhouse - as I have related to readers in my previous diary. They lived in the centre of town and Robbie had rarely ventured out of the house at all, let alone seen the green grass that surrounded us all when he later joined our family. Initially being scared of this vast expanse of greenness, he soon found his paws, however, and from then on enjoyed the country life as opposed to the urban one. He did have a few misadventures and

I remember an experience he had when meeting up with two rather large birds in a tree! No, not horrendous macaws like Geronimo, but nevertheless, quite scary, noisy big black menacing looking birds.

2.10pm: I turned around, licked my rear for a few moments, and settled more comfortably. I like being comfy when I am thinking back - perhaps it helps the memory! Well, as I said, Robbie wasn't a country cat and trees were utterly alien to him when he first joined our family. One day, after a few months of getting used to the sight of green grass and various kinds of vegetation, we were all sunning ourselves in the garden. He suddenly wandered off and - to our surprise - began climbing up a fairly large tree that overhung the rockery where we all used to like positioning ourselves on warm rocks during the summer. On and on and up and up he clambered, until he was nearly at the top. However, the branches were beginning to bend a little and he became rather scared and so decided not to ascend any further. He settled himself into the crook of some branches and made himself comfortable. However, he felt something sharp sticking into his back, so he turned around and found it was quite a large bird nest - though Robbie didn't realise what it was at the time, never having seen a bird nest before. He probably thought it was a platform conveniently placed there for cats to rest on! So he sat there for half an hour or so, quite comfy and surveying the world from his vantage point, whilst I, Tansy and Taro were spread out in the rockery below. Suddenly there was a load of rustling and squawking followed by a howl from Robbie. The owners of the nest had returned! They looked like a pair of large, untidy black crows or rooks, or perhaps jackdaws, I wasn't sure - they all look the same to me. Well, they were absolutely furious at finding a cat, of all creatures, sitting in their nest! They began flying at Robbie and grabbing bits of fur - anything their sharp beaks could reach! Robbie, now thoroughly frightened, tried to escape from the onslaught and get himself away. His paws were scrabbling at twigs and leaves - the latter showering down on we cats below - and he started to climb back down as fast as he could manage, bearing in mind that it was only his first time ever UP a tree. The two birds were verging on the edge of hysteria by now - thoroughly indignant at the nerve of a cat invading their nest. Well, from anyone's point of view, you have to see the funny side of it, don't you? A cat sitting in a bird nest! Robbie alighted in an undignified heap with the shrieks of the birds echoing in his ears. We ran up to him to see if he was okay, but apart from his ruffled fur and dignity he was just fine. Sheila arrived on the scene, wondering what all the rumpus was about, but once she had made sure that Robbie was unhurt she, too, saw the funny side of things and said she wished she'd had her little machine with her that takes pictures (another human gadget I just can't get my head around!) so that she could have recorded Robbie sitting on the nest for posterity! I tell you, dear reader, all the tales I have recounted to you in my diaries are true - you couldn't make up all the funny things that have happened to us in the past - and it certainly proves that the truth is funnier, or stranger, than fiction doesn't it?

Robbie at home in the birds nest

4.30pm: After my reminiscing about Robbie and the bird nest I fell asleep again, but now I gradually awoke and felt that a meal should be forthcoming - my tummy was beginning to grumble. Perhaps it was all those recollections about birds! I think I have forgotten to mention that in the past, apart from Geronimo the macaw about whom I have talked in length, Sheila and Peter have owned several birds - a white cockatoo called Pedro, two lovebirds called Bonnie and Clyde and two cockatiels called Tufty and Butch. I never saw any of these delectable creatures myself - perhaps just as well, because they would have been rather tempting to me when I was in my youth and at the top of my form at bird catching! Mind you, perhaps that's why you humans keep your pet birds behind bars - to protect them from cats. I don't think any of their other birds had particularly interesting personalities - give him his due, Geronimo certainly had one of those - so I've not had anything much to tell you about them. As far as I know, Pedro never really settled into captivity and he died relatively young for no known reason, Tufty and Butch just sat in their cage giving the odd chirp and whistle but never spoke, and Bonnie and Clyde just sat ogling each other all the time! Certainly nothing worth mentioning in my diaries!

6.45pm: Tummy now satisfied, I deposited myself on Sheila's knee as usual as she sat in her armchair in front of that hypnotic silver box. However, for once the front of it was black and no sounds seemed to be emanating from it. Perhaps there was nothing on it to whet their appetites this evening. She was holding one of those celebrity magazines she likes reading. I glanced over at Peter - he was in his usual sleep mode, so I guessed that pretty shortly he would start making those annoying roaring, whistling noises.

7.15pm: Yes, I was right - Peter was off! What a racket! I don't know how Sheila stands it. No way could I endure this, so I jumped off onto the floor and wandered out again into the kitchen. Nothing was left in the dinner bowl unfortunately. I resigned myself to a boring evening and was in the hall wondering whether to go upstairs to my comfy chair in Sheila's study or go back onto my mat in front of the patio door again, when suddenly a loud trumpeting nose sounded, which heralded the approach of visitors at the front door of the house. I ran back into the kitchen and peered round the door - I never like to show myself if any strange human enters the house unless I am quite sure I know them and where they've been. You can't be too careful as I've said before. Evidently Sheila and Peter knew these humans very well, but they obviously hadn't been expecting them. Chattering nineteen to the dozen, they seemed to fill the entire hall - quite alarming to a small cat-sized person - and I was glad I wasn't out there as I would quite likely have been trodden on!

8.00pm: Sheila and Peter and their two human friends, Sue and Tony, were by now sitting in their 'coffee corner' (an area off the dining room that Sheila calls the entertainment area), sipping the rather obnoxious-smelling stuff from tall glasses that all you humans seem to like. This, as I'm always saying is the ominous stuff that seems to send some humans silly and giggly and make others go to sleep or feel ill! Looks like water or pale brownish-coloured water to me, but obviously it must be stronger than water to affect them like it does. Cats sensibly stick to natural water, or sometimes milk, which is good for them and does not have the aforementioned adverse effects. Everyone seemed to be in good humour and they were making their awful laughing noises, and I felt rather left out to be honest. So I made my way into the area and, keeping at a safe distance, gave a perfunctory meow. The other humans immediately greeted me rather effusively saying, "Well, well, here's the famous author herself - come on Truffles, over here!" My mood immediately lightened - crumbs, they must have read my diaries! How very flattering - I hoped they had liked them! So I went over and received several pats and the lady human even picked me up and gave me a kiss. Pretty revolting I may say, but as she was obviously a fan I didn't struggle. I listened to their praises for a little while, but then withdrew and left them to their drinking session, deciding that I would sit out the rest of the evening in the study upstairs.

10.00pm: I had by now settled into the study chair, had my evening sleep and decided that I would try to recall just one more event to put in my diary which, hopefully, would amuse you all. Ah, yes! The tea party - or rather 'The Tea Party from Hell' as I heard Sheila describe it afterwards! I put my mind into reminiscing mode - this was going to be difficult to remember in its entirety as I was only a few months old at the time - Tansy and I had only been with the family for a comparatively short while. So I was trying to recall an episode that happened nineteen human years earlier. Best kept until tomorrow when I would have a clearer head, I thought - it was getting near my bedtime anyway. So, rather than remaining in the study, I made my way downstairs again.

10.05pm: The humans were still behaving in a rather undignified and stupid fashion, I thought, and I went in to see them in the hope that with a few stern looks from me they might soon become a bit quieter so that I could go to my bed and enjoy some peace and quiet. No chance! From sipping their drinks initially, they now seemed to be slurping them down at an alarming rate, their inane chatter was pretty well non-stop and the lady human visitor, Sue, was incessantly giggling with Sheila.

I watched them, fascinated. What a bad example of human decorum! We cats would never let ourselves behave in such a demeaning manner - we like to keep our dignity at all times. Peter and the other human, Tony, were almost as bad - their guffaws were in a lower key but still just as annoying to me. I marched in and stood in front of them so they couldn't miss seeing me. As I had hoped, they quietened down and Sue apologised if they had been disturbing or frightening me. "You see, Truffles," she said, "we haven't seen Sheila and Peter for such a long time and we are all such good friends that we have a lot to talk about and we are all so pleased to be with each other once again." I warmed to Sue - perhaps she was a compassionate person after all. I let her stroke my back a few times and then I rather pointedly yawned and started to walk away. They took the hint and became rather quieter. I left them to it and returned to the kitchen and my welcoming bed.

12.10pm: I had dozed off but was awakened by Sue and Sheila coming into the kitchen and making a lot of clatter washing up all their glasses and other bits and pieces - as I've said before, why on earth do you humans use so much crockery? All we cats need is one bowl for food and one for water and thus no dreary washing-up afterwards! By the tone of their conversation I gathered that Tony and Sue's motor machine was going to stay the night outside our house and they would stay inside the house - something to do with too much to drink I think they said. Eventually they all went upstairs and I was left to dream on for the rest of the night.

SATURDAY

9.30am: Lovely - no disturbance for me too early in the morning! I heard Sheila come down first - how amazing, as generally she never gets down before Peter! However, today she immediately got herself busy cooking up some nice-smelling bacon and eggs for their guests. I squirmed around her legs and, as anticipated, I was given several nice chunks of the bacon. To cook this delectable foodstuff, I note she doesn't use her magic box on the worktop but uses a kind of flat metal pan on the hob. Mmm, the smell of that cooking bacon in the pan made my mouth water and I hoped that I would be able to coerce her into giving me a few more bits later.

10.30am: Yes, I had been given some more bits of the bacon - nice and brown and crispy this time, and lip-smacking delicious! The humans had enjoyed their breakfast - again with much laughter and chattering. Does that Sue ever stop giggling? I asked myself. Peter had cleaned out my litter igloo and given me a cursory fur-do, and he, Sheila, Sue and Tony had retired outside to sit in the garden as once more it was a lovely day and the sun had his big hat on again. The humans all had those strange things called sunglasses covering their eyes. I've often wondered why you do that. Cats don't need such things - our eyes are clever enough to adjust themselves to different levels of light and dark. Still, of course, as I've always known, cats are the superior species all round - perhaps one day you humans will be able to measure up to us!

11.00am: Well, I promised you the story of the 'Tea Party from Hell' (depending on whether you looked at it from a human's or a cat's point of view) so here it is. As I said, Tansy and I were only very young at the time. Sheila had arranged a tea party outdoors in their big garden by the pond. She had invited about ten or so other humans and it was to celebrate some particular human event, but I don't know what - perhaps somebody's birthday. Sheila had worked very hard over the past day or so (something that must have been pretty alien to her I reckon!) but, yes indeed, she had produced two tables loaded with goodies - big plates of tasty-smelling pasties and pies, those strange things you humans call sandwiches, cakes, trifles - you name it, it was there. The tables were groaning under the weight of all the food, and alongside was another table loaded with a selection of the sickly-smelling drinks you all love. We cats were watching all this with great interest and plans were beginning to formulate in our minds as to how we were also going to make sure that we had a share of the tempting food - particularly those meat pies and pasties! Hennessy the clumsy St Bernard dog had been tied up on a long tether well away from the food area, as he had been known on several occasions in the past to have tipped whole tables of food over. Sheila was taking no chances on this occasion! In due course the other human guests arrived and for a half-hour or so all went well. They wandered around the garden, drinks in hand, admiring the flowers and chit-chatting generally. Eventually they all returned to the patio, congregated around the tables and started helping themselves to the goodies. Tansy could bear the temptation no more and, from a point in the rockery where we had all been sitting on high, she leapt suddenly onto the middle of the table, intending to grab a sausage roll. The following sequence of events seemed to happen in slow motion to everyone watching (both humans and we cats) though, in fact, it all took just a few seconds. Tansy, being young and inexperienced, misjudged the angle of her jump and, instead of landing in front of the plate of pies and sausage rolls as she had intended, she landed right in the middle of a very large bowl of trifle - splosh!

She was half immersed and the bowl, of course, tipped over, sending fruits, thick, glutinous yellow stuff and white creamy stuff spraying out in all directions. The humans screeched in unison and Tansy screeched even louder! Covered in cream, etc., she jumped off the table - still having the presence of mind to grab a sausage roll on the way - and collided immediately with a rather plump, elderly female human who was standing aghast just by the side of the table. Tansy's tail, covered in cream, swished all over this person's pristine, silky, lilac-coloured outer covering and at the same time Tansy knocked her handbag from her arm and it bounced and rolled over the patio until it hit the bank of the pond and fell right into the water. With the shock of all this, the lady human took a step backwards, cannoning into the person next to her, who overbalanced, couldn't save herself and also joined the first lady human's handbag in the pond! Well, talk about consternation in the camp! After an initial moment when all the humans seemed as though turned to stone, with one accord they moved to the pond and hauled out the unfortunate lady who had fallen in. Not only was she all wet, but also she had acquired a large plumage of pondweed, which had stuck to her head. The male humans who were still standing on the patio were hard pressed not to laugh, as, of course, were we cats who were still watching from our vantage points. Needless to say, Tansy had, not unsurprisingly, totally disappeared from the scene by this time! Well, I won't dwell on all the brouhaha that subsequently followed, but suffice to say that the party never really took off after that. The female who had fallen in the water left almost immediately and the other females remained pretty well subdued for the rest of the afternoon. However, the male humans seemed to enjoy the event hugely! Sheila wanted to wring Tansy's neck but was restrained from doing so!

Tansy's terror dive into the trifle!

1.30pm: Well, I had fallen asleep again - all this recollecting tires you out! All was peaceful here once more, as Sue and Tony had left in their motor machine to go back to their own home, which apparently was a long, long way away - certainly not in my beloved Cornwall - though I believe they did once live near here and that was how they had first met Sheila and Peter many years ago. Pity they had moved, I rather liked them ...

2.30pm: The sun continued to shine and I continued to sit in it. The rest of the day stretched out ahead - I was a happy cat ...

Goodbye from Truffles

Well, people, this is the end of my diary extracts - my third one now. I do hope you have enjoyed reading them and have seen things from my point of view that perhaps otherwise you wouldn't have known about.

My life is a good example of what a cat's life should be, isn't it? What more could any cat desire than to have a good human carer, or carers, whom you have been able to train to the highest level, plenty of good, nourishing food and a comfortable, warm home? I certainly don't want for anything and I believe that my longevity is due partly, of course, to my own astuteness and looking after myself carefully (always think of No. 1 first, that's my motto), but it is also due to the love and care that I have received from my own personal humans. I hope that we all have several more years together to come - so that we, human and feline, can continue to live together in harmony, with some humour and tolerance thrown in from both sides.

Kittenhood Memories ...

Synchronised whisker licking on the kitchen windowsill!

Hide and seek!

Nothing so tempting as a ball of wool!

THIS WAY UP!

Who wants a posh cat bed - give us a cardboard box any time!

The fishing party ...

Inspecting the birds house - must make sure they're comfortable!

www.apexpublishing.co.uk